MIDNIGHT MASSACRE

"All right, you Rebel bastards, jus' throw your hands up, right where you stand!" shouted the Yankee sergeant.

Marcus Quinn heard the metallic click of half a dozen rifles being cocked in the shadows.

"Get ready, boys," he whispered to his men as he raised his gun slowly.

In the pale moonlight, the dark shapes of six soldiers started materializing from behind the trees. They were armed with single-shot muzzleloaders.

"You Confederate trash is gonna pay for raidin' our armory. This here's an army ex'cution. Ready, men. Set—"

"Now!" Marcus yelled. His Colt .44 cleared leather in the next instant, blasting a hole in the sergeant's chest before he could finish his order.

Surprised and frightened, the rest of the soldiers fired wild, missing each man. Quinn and his Raiders never gave them a chance for a second shot.

When the thick cloud of gunsmoke cleared, seven soldiers lay dead in the dirt, cut down before they could even reload.

QUINN'S RAIDERS
Diablo Double Cross
J.D. Bodine

LYNX BOOKS
New York

QUINN'S RAIDERS: DIABLO DOUBLE CROSS

ISBN: 1-55802-035-7

First Printing/August 1988

This is a work of fiction. Names, characters, places, and incidents are either the product of the author's imagination or are used fictitiously. Any resemblance to actual events, locales, or persons, living or dead, is entirely coincidental.

Copyright © 1988 by the Jeffrey Weiss Group, Inc.
All rights reserved. No part of this book may be reproduced or transmitted in any form or by any means electronic or mechanical, including by photocopying, by recording, or by any information storage and retrieval system, without the express written permission of the Publisher, except where permitted by law. For information, contact Lynx Communications, Inc.

This book is published by Lynx Books, a division of Lynx Communications, Inc., 41 Madison Avenue, New York, New York, 10010. The name "Lynx" together with the logotype consisting of a stylized head of a lynx is a trademark of Lynx Communications, Inc.

Printed in the United States of America

0 9 8 7 6 5 4 3 2 1

QUINN'S RAIDERS
Diablo Double Cross

One

WHEN THE NORTHBOUND train stopped at Nacogdoches, Texas, it was met by a platform full of soldiers and civilians. The soldiers were dressed in Union blue. Although Robert E. Lee still had a fighting force in the field near a place called Appomattox, Virginia, the rest of the South had collapsed, and Nacogdoches was already adjusting to postwar conditions. Half a dozen entrepreneurs, down from the North, stood on the brick platform carrying their wares and belongings in carpetbags, waiting for the train to take them to new places of opportunity.

Three veterans of the Confederacy in dirty-gray uniforms sat on an unused baggage cart, watching the activity. One of the soldiers had an empty sleeve, another an empty trouser leg, and all three had empty spirits.

A couple of black men, "freed" by the war, were earning a few pennies by carrying baggage or loading cargo on the train. A wagon carrying three kegs of gunpowder stopped at the platform.

"Here, you, nig'ra. You want to make some money?"

One of the blacks looked toward the man who called them—a red-faced, well-dressed, heavyset civilian.

"Yes, sir."

"Load these here three kegs of gunpowder onto that last car there."

"Hold on," an army captain called out. "You can't load that powder in that car. That's where my men'll be riding."

"Sorry, Cap'n," the civilian said, showing the captain some papers. "That's the rules of the Kansas and Texas Railroad. They won't carry gunpowder in the baggage car."

"But it's only three kegs."

"That don't make no difference. They won't carry no amount a'tall."

"All right," the captain said after reading the papers. He handed them back to the civilian. "But they'll be hearing from the colonel soon as I reach Fort Leavenworth."

"You tell your colonel. Tell him to write 'em a good letter." The civilian chuckled. He signaled to the black man, who started loading the kegs of powder onto the passenger car at the end of the train.

"I seen 'em," a young boy shouted, running up to the platform. "I seen 'em comin'."

"You seen who, boy?" one of the carpetbaggers asked.

"I seen Quinn's Raiders," the boy said excitedly. "They got 'em in chains in a wagon. They're comin' this way."

"Quinn's Raiders?" one of the other carpetbaggers asked, moving over to the edge of the platform. "They're comin' here?"

"Who's Quinn's Raiders?" a third man asked.

"Who's Quinn's Raiders? Why, where was you durin' the war? They was just about the most ferocious fightin' unit in the whole war, that's all. You heard of Quantrill?"

"Yeah."

"Well, Quinn's Raiders made Quantrill's bunch seem like Sunday school teachers, is all."

"They prisoners of war?"

"No such a thing. I seen it in the paper last week. They're goin' to a civilian prison up North. It'll be a hundred years before any of those boys breathe free air again—if'n they don't swing first."

A wagon arrived at the edge of the platform and a squad of blue-clad soldiers jumped down. Holding their rifles at port arms, they watched five men, bound together by a heavy iron chain climb down from the wagon.

The prisoners were dressed in Confederate gray. One of them had the three gold stripes of a sergeant on his sleeve, another the three gold bars of a captain on his collar. The captain was tall and slim, blond, with blue eyes. The sergeant had dark hair, dark, brooding eyes, and a mustache that looked as if it were normally well trimmed, though all five of the men were in need of a shave.

"Answer when your name is called," a Union officer said.

"Marcus Quinn?"

"Yeah," the blond captain said.

"Hank Proudy?"

"At your service, sir," the dark, handsome prisoner said.

"Billy Joe Higgins."

"Here, Cap'n." Higgins was a big man, six feet five, well over two hundred pounds, with shoulders the width of an ax handle. He had red shaggy hair and beard, blue eyes, and freckles on his muscular arms.

"Bob Depro."

"Yep," Bob called out. He had dark hair, dark eyes, prominent cheekbones, and was of average height.

"And you'd be Loomis Depro?" The Union captain said to the last prisoner.

Loomis was dark, like his brother, but there the similarity ended. He was the youngest of the group, and short. He just nodded.

"All right, you men, get into the last car there."

On board the train the prisoners were seated in two facing wooden benches. An iron bar ran across the floor between them. Their chain was unlocked, passed through the bar, then locked again.

"Now you boys get real comfortable," the Union sergeant said, jerking on the chain so that the leg irons dug deep into their legs. Loomis grunted in pain. "But not too comfortable," the sergeant added, laughing as he moved to the front of the car to join his comrades.

There were four Union soldiers in the car to guard five prisoners. There were no other passengers in the car, though there were three kegs of gunpowder stacked up front.

"Who's got the cards?" the sergeant asked as he sat down with the others. By the time the train rolled out of the station with a series of jerks and squeaks, the soldiers were totally engrossed in their card game. No one was paying any attention to the five prisoners.

Marcus Quinn just sat there watching the Yankees and thinking. He'd heard on the ride up that the Union commander got special permission to hold him and the boys as civilian prisoners, not prisoners of war. That meant even if the war ended tomorrow, they'd swing for sure.

Only if Marcus had his way, he didn't intend to get as far as the federal prison for the trial. He had noticed that one of the bolts holding the iron bar retaining plate was loose. He nodded to Billy Joe and the big man started working on it.

By the time the train was twenty miles north of Nacogdoches, Billy Joe had worked the bolt loose. After that it was easy to slip the chain out from under the bar but they were still bound together by their legs, and their wrists were secured by manacles.

Bob nodded and Quinn turned to look toward the front of the car where the soldiers were playing cards.

"Sergeant?" he called.

"Yeah?" he answered without looking up.

"Spare a cigar?"

"A cigar? Now what makes you think I would give a cigar to Confederate trash like you?"

"I can pay for it."

"Yeah? How? We searched you, and you ain't got a copper cent."

"No, but I got some money buried."

That caught the sergeant's interest.

"I'm listening."

"Hell, Sergeant, we hit near fifteen or twenty trains and money shipments during the war," Marcus said. "We got money hid all over Texas, Kansas, Missouri, and Arkansas."

"Keep talking."

Marcus chuckled. "How about a cigar?"

"What if you're lyin'?"

"I guess you just got to trust me," Marcus said, smiling.

"Mister, I ain't simple enough to think you'd tell me where you hid all your money just for a cigar."

"Oh, I ain't tellin' you where I hid *all* of it. Just a little, like a few hundred dollars from a little job we did a couple of months ago near Henderson. When we stop for water you could jump off the train and get the money. If I'm lyin', why, you can settle with me when you get back on."

The sergeant smiled. "All right, you tell me, I'll look for it, and if I find it, I'll give you a cigar."

"Well," Marcus said, "suppose I tell you and you don't give me the cigar. Ain't nothin' I can do about it."

"That's sounds fair, Sarge," one of the other soldiers said.

"Shut up. I'm makin' the decision here," the sergeant said.

"Shit, if you ain't gonna give 'im a cigar, I will."

"No you ain't," the sergeant growled. "It's my deal."

"Don't you boys worry about it," Marcus said. "Ol' sarge here looks like a sharin' man. Else you'd set to talkin' . . ."

"Damn you," the sergeant said. "Keep your damn mouth shut."

"He didn't tell us nothin' we ain't already been thinkin' about," one of the soldiers said.

"All right," the sergeant said. "Here's your damn cigar, but you only get one for the lot of you. I ain't comin' up with five of 'em."

"One's all we need," Marcus said.

The sergeant walked back and put the cigar in Marcus's mouth, then lit it. Marcus took several puffs, letting each puff out in a loud, satisfied sigh. Finally, when a substantial cloud of blue smoke had been raised, he reached up with his manacled hands and pulled the cigar out of his mouth to pass it to Hank.

"Now where's that money?" the sergeant asked.

"When we stop for water, go to the northeast leg of the water tank," Marcus said. "Look up under the bottom of the tank and you'll see a shelf. The money's in a burlap bag on that shelf."

"How much is there?" the sergeant asked eagerly.

"Well, Sergeant, this just may be the most expensive cigar I ever smoked," Marcus said. "As near as I can recall, there's six hundred and fifty-four dollars in that bag."

"Sumbitch!" the sergeant said, smiling broadly. "Think of that, boys. Over six hundred dollars."

The sergeant went back to the front to rejoin the others. They continued the card game, though their conversation dealt entirely with what they were going to do with the money once they got it.

"Marcus, ain't no money there," Billy Joe whispered.

"Don't matter. We'll be long gone."

"You got a plan?"

"Yeah. Give me the cigar."

Marcus took several puffs on the cigar until the end was glowing cherry red. He looked toward the front, and seeing that the Yankee soldiers were engrossed in their card game and conversation, he flipped the cigar toward the three kegs of gunpowder. The cigar landed on the cracked top of the nearest keg.

For a minute nothing happened.

"It caught," Loomis said. "I can see smoke."

"We'll give it ten seconds," Marcus said, "then we got to duck behind these seats."

"Marcus, that's three kegs. We might all get blowed to hell," Hank said.

"We might at that," Marcus said, smiling broadly.

Slowly and quietly, Marcus counted. When he reached ten, he yelled, "Now!"

The five men stood up quickly and jumped around behind the wooden bench Billy Joe, Bob, and Loomis had been sitting on.

"What the hell?" the Yankee sergeant shouted, rising to his feet then. "They're gettin' away!" The Yankee sergeant fired at them, the bullet crashing through the back of the seat, then through the window.

"Goddamn!" Hank shouted. "When's that son of a bitch gonna blow?!"

Suddenly one of the Yankee soldiers saw the smoke curling up from the gunpowder.

"Sarge, look out!"

"Shit!" the Yankee sergeant shouted, and he started toward the window.

It was too late. At that moment the powder went off with a blinding flash and a deafening roar. The front half of the car where the soldiers were was completely blown away, leaving the back half slanting down toward the track bed from the rear wheels. The back of the car was filled with smoke from the charge. The train had been running at better than thirty miles per hour when the gunpowder exploded, so the severed car continued under its own momentum for a while before coming to a rough stop. The main body of the train went on for several hundred feet before the engineer realized what had happened. He applied the brakes, bringing the train to a screeching, dead stop.

All five of the boys were coughing furiously, trying to clear their throats, nostrils, and eyes of the acrid cordite. When the smoke cleared, Marcus looked around the car. It was as if some giant had cut it in two with an ax. The front half was gone and so were the Yankee soldiers.

"You boys all right?"

Each of his men answered him in the affirmative.

"Come on, we got to get out of here before the train backs up," he said.

"We ain't goin' to move very fast like this," Hank grumbled, rattling his chains.

"Don't matter. Ain't nobody left on the train but civilians and they sure as hell ain't goin' to be comin' after us. They'll prob'ly head on to Henderson, then telegraph back askin' what to do next."

The Raiders jumped out of the open end of the car, then ran down the coal-and-cobble-covered berm to hide in some brush by the track. They watched as the train backed up. Several people got off the train and ran up to the wreckage to look around.

"I said all along, you ain't got no business carryin' gunpowder on the same train as passengers," Marcus heard the conductor say.

"What you think caused it?" someone asked.

"Hell, it could'a been anything," the conductor said. "Maybe one of 'em was smokin'. Maybe a spark flew in from the engine. Who knows? All I know is nine men are dead."

"Nine?" Loomis asked.

Marcus held a finger to his lips.

"Well, if you ask me, it's good riddance for that Quinn and his men," the engineer put in. "I had my train stopped two times by them thievin' bastards."

"That's war," the conductor suggested.

"War hell. I suppose they took my watch and suspenders for the war, huh? They done it 'cause they liked doin' it. Come on, we got to get to Henderson and send a telegraph so they can get the track cleared."

The train crew and curious passengers reboarded the train and with several chugging puffs of steam, the train began rolling again. Quinn and the others waited for several moments until the sound of the train had faded in the distance. Now there was only the whisper of the wind and the flutter of grasshoppers. He stood up and looked at the chains.

"They think we're dead," Billy Joe said.

"I reckon that means they won't be lookin' for us."

"All we gotta do is get outta here."

"Yeah, well, how the hell we gonna do that? We can hardly even move with these damn chains on us."

"Then the thing to do is to find us a farm and get out of all this iron," Marcus said.

"Yeah, and maybe get something to eat," Billy Joe suggested.

"And some horses," Loomis added.

"We'll take whatever we need," Marcus agreed.

"Marcus, ain't we goin' back to headquarters?" Bob asked.

"Shit," Hank said, "you think them lyin' Texas bastards'll be there? After they set us up in a Yankee ambush to save their hides?"

"Maybe not," Billy answered, scratching his beard, "but the war ain't over yet and we's still in the army. Got to report somewhere."

Marcus was silent. He looked at his men and realized that after five long years of war, all they had to show for it was the tattered uniforms on their backs and the chains on their wrists and ankles.

"Boys," Marcus began, "you heard the conductor. It's just like Billy Joe said—we was killed when that powder blowed. Seems to me like we got nobody waitin' on us an' no place to go. I say we head West."

The men looked at one another, then broke into a loud cheer.

Two

IT WAS NO surprise that Marcus Quinn was the captain and the leader of Quinn's Raiders. The five young men had come together long before the war, and even then, Quinn had been the natural leader. Before the war, Marcus Quinn had been one of the most popular young men in Claiborne County, Mississippi. Life had been fun for Marcus and his friends. The nearest town was Bay Water, a rural settlement in the rich, black, bottomland of the bayous of the Mississippi Delta. It was farming country, and within two generations, great plantations were built and fortunes were made. Some of the farms were enormous, with thousands of acres under cultivation, and hundreds of slaves who worked the fields, tended the livestock, and catered to every whim of the gentlemen farmers and their families.

Not everyone in Claiborne County was rich, of

course, but most of the families did own slaves, even the smaller farmers. Marcus Quinn and those who rode with him were no exception.

Marcus was a person whom most people couldn't figure out. People had only good to say about Marcus. As a boy he had been an acolyte in St. Paul's Episcopal Church, and during one communion service when Marcus carried the cross down the aisle, sporting a black eye and cut lip, everyone felt sorry for this little blond boy who was set upon by some ruffian. Few knew that the other boy in the fight suffered much more than a black eye and a cut lip. Marcus had bitten the other boy's ear lobe off, twisted two fingers until they were broken, and left a scar on the boy's cheek that would be with him for the rest of his life.

People said that Marcus could charm the birds right out of the trees. And the ones who knew him hoped for better things than to see him steal whiskey from the stills over in Copiah County, or get himself mixed up in a duel with Arnaud Mouchette, the son of the lieutenant governor of Louisiana.

Mouchette had demanded the duel, an "affair of honor," he called it, and the two met one misty morning on a Louisiana road amidst cypress knees and brown pelicans. Mouchette hurried his shot and Marcus heard the bullet go by, the shock wave of its passage popping in his ear. Marcus fired a split second later and saw an ugly, black hole appear in Mouchette's chest. Mouchette covered the hole with his hand, then stood there with a look of surprise on his face as the blood spilled through his fingers, and fell.

He was the first man Marcus had ever killed. Marcus looked at the dueling pistol in his hand, and with a grunt of disgust, threw it into the bayou. He had killed many men since then, but Marcus could still remember riding away that morning, with Mouchette lying dead on the ground behind him.

Of the group who surrounded Quinn, Hank Proudy's family was the wealthiest. Hank's father, Martin, owned Trailback, one of the finer plantations in the county. But Hank had an older brother and a younger sister, and he never quite found his place among the genteel folk of the county. He much preferred the company of Marcus Quinn and the others, spurning the social contacts his father had cultivated for him.

At the barbeques and cotillions, or over bourbon and branch on the verandas of elegant homes, the "quality" people of Claiborne County often discussed the strange case of Hank Proudy. Most agreed that Hank was a young man who had everything going for him—a fine family, good looks, excellent social contacts, and a good mind. But they also agreed that despite everything, he was a lost cause and a ne'er-do-well.

"My brother is no damned good," Clay Proudy said of Hank, speaking with ill-concealed disdain. "There are some people who are born to be bad, and Hank is one of them."

"That boy is going to hang someday," Hank's father said. "It's a hell of a thing to say about your own flesh and blood, but if ever there was a man born to hang, it's Hank."

Billy Joe Higgins's father was a wild Irishman who

some say left Ireland to escape the hangman after breaking a man in two. Like his father, Billy Joe was a powerful man who could use his strength to save someone, but he also went over to Hinds County once and single-handedly whipped the sheriff and three of his deputies. He didn't go just to pick a fight, but to enjoy the county fair. But one of the Hinds County deputies was a bully who mistook Billy Joe's quiet demeanor for slowness of wit. The deputy picked the fight and even with two other deputies and the sheriff fighting at his side, Billy Joe whipped them.

Bob and Loomis Depro were one-half Choctaw Indian. Loomis, the youngest and smallest of the entire group, was an excellent horseman who could be counted on to win any horse race he entered. There was nothing about horses or any other animal illnesses that he didn't know.

Loomis was very good with a knife. After a disputed finish to a horse race held in Arkansas, Loomis got into a knife fight. The other man was older and bigger than Loomis, and he was raised in the Arkansas hill country where he cut his teeth on a long, slim knife that folks called an "Arkansas toothpick."

Despite his age and experience, young Loomis got the better of the fight, cutting his adversary up pretty good, and leaving an awful scar and a drooping eyelid on the other man's face. Loomis showed then that he was as quick and agile as a cat and very few people made the mistake of ever underestimating him again.

Before both boys were twenty, their father died. Shortly after that a group of night riders came out to the farm to try and frighten the Indian woman and her two half-breed children into leaving the county.

However, they hadn't reckoned on the Depro boys, especially Bobby's lightning-fast bullwhip. With a few quick but precise moves, he had them off their horses and their weapons scattered fifty yards away, useless. By the time the hapless riders were able to remount and run, their blood-soaked shirts were in threads and their backs raw from lashes. They never bothered the Depro place again.

Each of these men was more than anyone could handle, but together there wasn't a local lawman or irate husband in the whole state of Mississippi who'd dare go up against them. Marcus and the boys raised more hell than Claiborne County had seen in many years. When the war broke out, and the boys signed up to fight for the South as a unit, most folks heaved a sigh of relief. With Marcus and his friends wearing gray, the Yankees wouldn't stand a chance.

And they were close to right. Once the Confederate Army realized that these boys could do more damage to the Yankees as a freewheeling guerrilla team instead of regular soldiers, they made Marcus captain and ordered them to do what they did best: raise hell any way they could against the North. Stealing supplies, bushwhacking troops, blowing up trains, robbing payrolls—Quinn's Raiders became the most hated and effective small fighting unit in the South.

Marcus and his boys got used to taking whatever they wanted—no matter which side of the law they were on.

Three

APPROXIMATELY TEN MILES away from where Quinn and the others had blasted themselves free of the train, a gray-haired old black man known only as Targo sat on a wooden bench in a small shack behind a large white house. In the shack with him a coffin rested on a couple of sawhorses in the middle of the room. Lying in the coffin was the body of Colonel Nathan J. Culpepper. Targo had prepared the body so that the colonel's gray mustache and beard were neatly trimmed, and the gray hair was carefully groomed in such a way as to cover up his head wound. Targo had dressed him, too, and although Culpepper had been a colonel in the Confederate Army, Targo chose to dress the man who had been his master in the uniform of a colonel in the army of the Republic of Texas, for it was in that uniform that Nathan Culpepper had won glory on the fields of San

Jacinto in the battle for Texas independence.

The old black man, who was approximately the same age as his one-time master, had been with Colonel Culpepper when he built this ranch forty years ago, had left it to go to war against Mexico with him, and was at his side at San Jacinto when Sam Houston beat Santa Anna. He had also been at Colonel Culpepper's side six hours ago when the colonel suddenly and without warning put a pistol to his own head and blew his brains out.

The unexpected action had left Targo confused, and he spent most of the afternoon and early evening trying to figure out what he should do next.

Targo heard a crashing sound from the main house, then a loud shriek of woman's laughter. He looked toward it in disgust, thinking of the new owner and the white-trash whore who had come to live with him. When the new owner learned of Colonel Culpepper's suicide, he dismissed it with an impatient wave of his hand.

"Do whatever you want to do," he'd said, "then leave. You're a free nigger now. I don't need you around here. In fact, I don't want you around here. Bury that old fool somewhere tonight and be gone by morning."

Being chained together made it hard to walk, and even more difficult to hide when they heard or saw riders. If someone happened onto five men chained together by leg irons and cuffed at the wrists, there would be some necessary explanations. Therefore,

DIABLO DOUBLE CROSS

Marcus and the others spent most of the day jumping into ditches or hiding behind bushes.

Night had fallen by the time they came across a place they thought might have the tools they needed to break free. By the light of the moon, they could see a big ranch, complete with a main house, bunkhouse, stables, and most important to their needs, a blacksmith shed. The upstairs of the big house was ablaze with bright lights, but the downstairs, as well as the bunkhouse, was completely dark. They listened intently, but there was no sound save the raucous chorus of insects and occasional restless snorting of a horse. Quietly the boys slipped through the night shadows until they reached the blacksmith shed. They opened a creaking door and stepped inside. There was a metallic clank.

"Ouch!" Loomis said.

"Watch it," his brother warned.

"Watch what? I can't see nothin'," Loomis complained.

"Billy Joe, it's darker than a witch's ass. How are you goin' to find the tools?" Hank asked.

"I don't need no light," Billy Joe declared. "I was raised in a blacksmith shed. I can find what I need by feel."

A long table was built alongside one wall. The table was filled with tools, scrap iron, nuts and bolts, and bits of leather. Billy Joe fumbled around, clanking and thumping through the loose objects, until he found what he was looking for.

"I've got it," he said. "A hammer and chisel. Put your hands up here on the anvil, Marcus."

"You sure you know what you're doing?" Marcus asked, raising his hands as directed.

There was a loud ping, and Marcus's hands were free. He held both of them up to show his success.

"Good job, Billy Joe," Marcus said. Hank put his wrists across the anvil and Billy Joe popped the lock pin with one blow. He finished all the wrist manacles and was about to hand the hammer and chisel to Marcus, when Marcus stopped him.

"What?" Billy Joe asked.

Marcus didn't answer him. Instead, he spoke into the shadows in the corner of the shed.

"You there," he called in a low, menacing voice. "Come on out where I can see you or I'm gonna start blastin'."

There was a movement in the shadows, then a dark, nearly invisible shape took form. It was a man, difficult to see not only because of the darkness of the shed, but also because the man was black.

"No, sir," the man said. "I don't reckon you gonna do no blastin', 'cause you ain't got nothin' to blast with. I got me this here shotgun and could do some blastin' o' my own, iffen I was of the mind."

"You couldn't get us all. Try it and one of us'll wrap a length of chain around your neck," Bob growled.

"I said iffen I was of a mind," the black man repeated. "I don't reckon to do no shootin', no way." The blacksmith put the gun down, leaning it against the work bench.

"Who are you, boy?" Marcus asked.

"My name's Targo. I used to be the blacksmith on this here place. I worked here for near forty years."

"This a ranch?"

"This here place is called Hillcrest Ranch. It was built by Colonel Nathan Culpepper. I reckon you heard of him. He was with Sam Houston at San Jacinto," the blacksmith said proudly.

"Yeah," Hank said. "I heard of him."

Marcus tried to open Billy Joe's cuffs, but he lacked the big man's skill.

"'Scuse me, I'll do this," Targo said.

The black man took the hammer and chisel from Marcus, then, with one swing of the hammer, knocked the cuffs off.

"Obliged," Billy Joe said. He took the hammer and chisel back, then started to work on the leg irons.

"Mister, I got me a punch," Targo suggested. "You might have better luck poppin' them leg irons with a punch. I ought to know. I done popped enough of 'em offen runaway slaves."

"You said you used to be the blacksmith. You still working for the colonel?"

"Not no more, no, sir. This here ranch don't belong to Colonel Culpepper no more. It got took away from him last week."

"Took away?"

"Some Yankee gennel'man come down carryin' a carpetbag in one hand and a piece of paper in the other. The paper says this here ranch belongs to him now." The huge, dark shape stepped over to the table. He moved a few tools around, then picked up the punch. He reached for the hammer, which Billy Joe returned without question.

"Where's Colonel Culpepper now?"

"I buried 'im this evenin', 'bout an hour ago," Targo said. He put the punch on the retaining pin and hit it with the hammer. The pin popped out and the leg iron opened. He moved to the next cuff.

"Yankee bastards kill him?" Hank asked.

"Well, sir. The colonel's two boys was both kilt in the war. His wife took sick an' died an' I reckon there weren't nothin' left for him but this here ranch. When the Yankees took that, too, why, the ol' gennel'man didn't have nothin' left to live for. He up an' blowed his brains out."

As he told the story of his dead master, he moved from cuff to cuff quickly and skillfully. Within two minutes all five men were free of their bonds.

"Thanks, Targo," Marcus said.

"You gennel'mens'll be wantin' horses and saddles?"

"We come a long way walkin'," Marcus answered.

"The colonel owned a string of the best-blooded animals in East Texas. And saddles a' plenty. You'll find 'em in the barn."

"Why are you doing this for us?"

"First place, I just natural feel for any man that's in chains," Targo explained. "An' I ain' got nothin' but hate in my heart for the Yankee that took this place over an' caused the colonel to kill hisself. So I been studyin' on it, an' I was thinkin' on pickin' out one of the colonel's horses for myself an' runnin' the rest of 'em off just so's the carpetbagger wouldn't have 'em. I reckon lettin' you have 'em is just as good."

"Well, amen to that. Now are any more guns around here?" Marcus asked.

"Just this here old ten-gauge Greener goose gun is all."

"A shotgun. That's no good."

"Wait a minute," Hank put in. He rubbed his chin for a moment. "I'll take it. You know I can't shoot worth a damn. Shotgun's just what I need."

"It's too long to carry around."

"Hell, Targo can fix that."

Targo smiled and his teeth could be seen shining in the dark.

"Mister, I cut that gun, you gonna have yourself some kind of a killin' weapon," he noted.

"We got to get some more guns," Bob said.

Targo walked over to where he left the shotgun. He brought it back to the vise, then started sawing the barrel.

"Well, sir, you could try the armory over to Minden," Targo suggested. "I hear that's where the Yankee army put all the guns they stole from the 'Federate soldiers."

The Minden Armory was a large white-painted building at the eastern edge of town. It was well after midnight, and not one light shone from any of the buildings along the sides of the single street. The armory doors were padlocked and the windows barred, but there were no guards standing by the doors. The boys tied their horses to a stand of cottonwood trees near the northeast corner of the armory.

Out on the prairie a coyote howled.

Somewhere in the town a dog answered the coyote's howl.

A weather vane squeaked as it twisted with a freshening breeze.

An owl hooted.

"Loomis," Marcus whispered. "Move all the way around the building for a look-see."

Without a word Loomis started around the building, running swiftly in a low crouch, darting from shadow to shadow. He went all the way around the building, returning a couple of minutes later.

"Nobody."

Marcus smiled. "All right, boys, what do you say we help ourselves?"

Billy Joe had brought a crowbar from the blacksmith shed. He put the bar through the hasp of the lock and broke it open with one pull. After that it was just a matter of opening the door and walking inside.

Marcus found a lantern and lit it, then let out a low whistle. The armory was full of all kinds of weapons, from captured field artillery pieces to Gatling guns. There were hundreds of rifles and pistols of every size and caliber, as well as pikes, swords, bayonets, knives, and dirks. There were crates upon crates of ammunition, and even cases of tinned beef, hard tack, and peaches.

"Marcus, look," Hank said. "Here's a bunch of Colt Forty-four Navys already converted for metal ammunition."

The Colt Navy was the gun Marcus most preferred. It was simple, rugged, beautifully balanced, and in the hands of an expert, extremely accurate. The .44-caliber bullet weighed 216 grains, and the thirty grains of black powder gave it a deadly punch.

Marcus started through the pistols, hefting several to test their balance and feel until he found one that suited him.

The Colt was a single-action pistol, which meant that cocking had to be done by hand. But that didn't present a problem for someone like Marcus, who was so expert at the quick draw that cocking was an intregal part of the drawing action. By the time the pistol was lined up for firing, the chamber would be in line with the barrel, ready to fire.

Marcus was not only the natural leader of the bunch; he had also proven to be the most skilled with a handgun, drawing and firing so quickly that most opponents saw only smoke.

Each of the others strapped on Colt .44s, but they also looked for additional weapons to give them an edge. Hank, who already had a sawed-off Greener, also found a small four-barrel .22-caliber Sharps. This pistol could be hidden in the palm of his hand. Also called a belly gun, or holdout, it was the type of weapon that Hank liked to have handy. Belly guns weren't accurate beyond ten feet, though over the space of a poker table they could be quite deadly.

"Hey, look at this!" Billy Joe said, smiling broadly as he held up a Mare's Leg. The Mare's Leg, sometimes called a horse pistol, was often referred to as a portable cannon. Though not much larger than a pistol, the gun fired a heavy .58-caliber shell with enough impact power to tear a door off its hinges or knock a hole in a brick wall. It took a big man to handle such a weapon, and it was the weapon Billy Joe carried with him all during the war.

Loomis strapped on a bowie knife. The agile youngster had proven his ability with the weapon time and time again.

They each took a Henry rifle as well, of which it was said one could "load it on Sunday and shoot it all week."

"All right," Marcus said as they slipped the rifles into the saddle holsters and tied on the bags of ammunition. "We've got everything we need. Let's get out of here."

"What about some grub?" Billy Joe asked.

"Yeah, I could do with a can of those peaches," Loomis put in.

"We been here too long now," Marcus replied. "If anyone saw the lantern . . ."

"Come on, Marcus, ain't nobody even awake," Hank said.

Marcus looked all around the building, searching the shadows. "All right," he agreed. "Fill a couple of sacks and then let's get the hell out of here."

"Man, I can taste the peaches now," Loomis said excitedly.

"Loomis, you stay here and hold the horses," Marcus ordered. "We'll get the food."

"Sure thing, Marcus, but be sure and get some—"

"Hard tack, right? Ain't that what you're wantin', little brother?" Bob teased.

Marcus, Hank, Billy Joe, and Bob went back to the armory and started filling two burlap bags with tins of food while Loomis waited outside.

"All right," Marcus whispered a few moments later. "We've got what we need. Let's go."

Loomis led the horses over to the door, and they were just throwing the bags across the saddles when someone called to them from the darkness.

"All right, you Rebel bastards, jus' throw your hands up, right where you stand!"

Marcus heard half a dozen metallic clicks as rifles were cocked in the shadows.

"Get ready, boys," Marcus whispered. He put his hands up, then called out loudly. "Who's there?"

In the pale moonlight, shapes began materializing from the trees, and a moment later Marcus saw a Yankee sergeant with six soldiers. The sergeant, about six feet two, with a long brown beard, was holding a pistol pointed at the boys. The soldiers with him were holding rifles. The rifles were, Quinn noted, single-shot muzzleloaders.

"I seen your lantern," the sergeant said. "So I got me a squad and come on down here to see what was going on." The sergeant squirted a brown stream of tobacco juice, then wiped his chin. He smiled, showing yellow-brown teeth. "I reckon when the cap'n sees the bodies of you five secesh in the mornin', me an' all the boys here'll be gettin' a little reward. On my order, boys."

The soldiers started to raise their rifles.

"Now!" Quinn shouted, and his pistol was in his hand as fast as his shout. He shot the sergeant first, hitting him right between the eyes. The sergeant died with the evil smile still on his face, never even realizing that he was in danger.

The soldiers fired, but just as Marcus had figured, they were surprised and frightened, and hurried their shots so that not one of the bullets struck flesh. The soldiers didn't get a chance for a second shot because Quinn's Raiders cut them down in a blaze of gunfire.

Thick gunsmoke formed a billowing cloud, then drifted away from the scene as the echoes of the shots rolled back from a distant stand of trees. A nearby dog began to bark and a dozen others in the town took up the chorus.

"What was that?" a voice shouted from the back of one of the houses.

"It came from the armory," someone answered.

"Let's get the hell out of here," Marcus growled, thrusting his smoking pistol down in the holster. "Load up your guns, men. We're gonna ride outta here, makin' these folks think all the demons from hell are comin' through."

"Demons from hell. Shit, that's what we are, ain't we?" Loomis asked with a laugh.

The five men mounted, not bothering to look at the seven bodies their carnage had left dead. Slapping their legs against the sides of their horses, they started down the main street of the town at a gallop.

"Yahoo!" Marcus shouted, and he was joined by the others as they gave the shout that during the war became known as the "Rebel yell." Marcus fired at the windows and doors of the buildings to discourage anyone who might have an idea of ambushing them.

Two blasts from the double-barrel Greener took out four windows in front of the hardware store. Billy Joe's Mare's Leg roared and a corner support post for the front porch of the marshal's office was shot away. The roof caved in on the front of the building, trapping everyone inside. Not one shot was fired in return. When the boys had gone a mile and then turned to look back, they saw that no one was making any effort to follow them.

Marcus smiled broadly. They were free, mounted, and armed. The whole West lay before them.

Four

TWO DAYS AFTER the shootout at the Minden Armory, Marcus and his group were five miles east of Hempstead, Texas. They stopped there to let the horses rest and drink from a stream that ran alongside the road. Loomis began tossing pebbles into the stream while Bob put the finishing touches to a bullwhip he had fashioned from strips of leather he took from the Hillcrest Ranch. Billy Joe lay on the bank of the stream with a straw in his mouth. Hank and Marcus climbed up the little embankment to the road.

"I've never been so goddamned broke I didn't have two coins to rub together," Hank complained. "Marcus, we don't have two cents between the lot of us."

"Yep," Marcus said.

"I'd like to be able to go into town and buy a drink or two. Maybe get some more duds and say hello to a pretty woman."

"You got any ideas?" Marcus wanted to know.

"Well, hell, there's bound to be a bank in Hempstead," Hank said.

"Yeah, let's hit the son of a bitch," Bob said.

"Count me in," Loomis said.

"How about you, Billy Joe?"

"All right by me, Marcus."

"Boys, there's better ways of raisin' money than robbin' a bank," Marcus said. "Banks are right in the middle of town and all. But right now, I don't see no other opportunity."

"When?"

"No time like the present," Marcus said as he got mounted.

"Yeah, well, let's do it," Hank agreed.

Hempstead, Texas, was a busy little town, built around a square. Half a dozen wagons were parked along the streets. The board sidewalks were full of men and women, farmers and ranchers, looking in the windows, hurrying to and fro.

"Is this Saturday?" Marcus asked.

"Hell, I don't know. I don't keep no calendar," Hank answered.

"Too many damn people in town," Billy Joe said.

"Maybe that's to the good, Billy. More people in the way so we can get away easy," Bob suggested.

"Maybe," Marcus said, though his voice sounded as if he didn't really believe it. "There's the bank."

"How much you reckon's in it?"

"I don't know," Marcus said. "Town this small . . . maybe five hundred to a thousand dollars."

* * *

Diablo Double Cross

Inside the bank at that moment, though the boys weren't aware of it, two hundred thousand dollars had just been deposited. The money belonged to the Gulf and Northern Railroad, and to protect their money, they had four armed Pinkerton men inside the bank and four more at strategic locations outside. Two of the guards inside were posing as bank clerks, the other two as farmers. They were experienced men, and when they saw five riders stop in front of the bank, but only two come in, they were on the alert.

Marcus was glad there were no women in the bank. If there was going to be shooting, he didn't want to worry about killing any women. He and Hank went inside. Hank had the sawed-off Greener under his coat, Marcus had his hand on his Colt .44. As soon as they were inside, Marcus pulled his pistol.

"This here's a holdup," he called. "You, teller, empty out your bank drawer and put all the money in a bag."

"Pinkerton men! Throw down your guns!" yelled one of the men Marcus had thought was a farmer.

Marcus swung his pistol toward the man who had yelled at him. The detective fired first. His bullet hit an inkwell on one of the tables, sending up a spray of ink. Quinn returned fire and his bullet found its mark. Hank let off a blast with his sawed-off shotgun and the shaded glass around the teller cages shattered as the men behind the counter dropped to the floor. One of them fired back and his bullet cut a hole in Hank's jacket.

"Let's get the hell out of here!" Marcus yelled,

pulling Hank with him and firing back into the bank as they ran out front.

The four Pinkerton men outside had heard the shooting and now joined the fray. One of them was on the roof of the building opposite the bank. He opened up with a shotgun but since he was out of range of all the boys, they were merely hit with pellets that barely penetrated the skin. Another guard on a different roof fired and the front window of the bank came crashing down. A third guard killed Hank's horse just as Hank got to it. Loomis offered his stirrup to Hank, who mounted while Billy Joe, firing his Mare's Leg, took out one guard. Marcus saw a man kneeling behind a water trough, taking slow and deliberate aim with a Winchester. Marcus fired and the man fell forward, his unfired rifle sinking in the water.

The boys started toward the end of the street at a gallop, then saw that several men had turned over one of the wagons to use as a barricade against them.

"This way!" Loomis shouted, and he rode straight toward two men preparing to install the plate-glass window of a half-built dressmaking shop. He urged his horse forward and the horse leaped through the open space, clearing the way for the other three horses who followed close behind.

They clattered across the wooden floor, then through the back to the outside, onto an open field. It was a brilliant move. None of the townspeople were mounted, and by the time they did reach their horses and come around the edge of town, the Raiders had completely disappeared.

The boys rode hard for nearly half an hour before

Diablo Double Cross

they came to a road. Behind a little hill just to the side of the road, they stopped to let the horses recover their wind. Marcus took roll to learn that, except for a few stings from the buckshot, no one was hurt.

"Damn," Hank said. "Those folks sure went to a lot of trouble just to protect a couple hundred dollars."

"I got an idea," Marcus said.

"What?"

"Next time we hit a bank, let's *plan* to hit it first. Now come on. We gotta get another horse and some money."

Later that day the opportunity for both presented itself when Bob, who had been standing lookout, came back to tell them that he had seen a coach coming down the road.

Marcus scrambled up to the top of a small hill, then looked around the curve of the road. He saw a coach-and-four pulled by matched white horses. The driver was wearing a red driving coat, and there were two footmen riding on the back. There was also a beautiful saddlehorse tied on to trail along behind. Marcus smiled broadly, then ran back down.

"Boys," he said, grinning from ear to ear, "unless I miss my guess, we got us a fat goose fallin' right into our laps."

The others came up to the side of the road. Marcus, Billy Joe, and Bob Depro stood on one side, Hank and Loomis on the other.

"Billy Joe," Marcus called, pointing to a tree limb about six feet long and six inches in diameter. "Move on down the road about fifteen feet. When the coach comes even with you, shove that in the wheels."

"Right," Billy Joe agreed. He picked up the tree limb and moved down the side of the road a short distance, then stepped out of sight.

Marcus could hear the driver's whistles and shouts as the coach continued down the road. It was close enough now for him to hear the clatter of horses' hooves and the rumble and squeak of the coach itself. Finally the vehicle appeared around the bend.

It was a beautiful coach, shiny green with silver scrollwork and highly polished brass sidelamps. Marcus watched it, then saw Billy Joe rise up from the side of the road, dart toward the coach, and thrust the pole into the wheels. The coach bucked and twisted and there was the crack of a busted spoke. The driver hauled back on the reins, not yet aware of what actually happened, and the coach lurched to a stop.

Marcus and the others stepped out into the road with their guns drawn.

"Here! What the hell is this?" the driver shouted.

"Step down off the box, mister," Marcus called. "You fellas get off the back."

The driver, who was white, and the two footmen, both of whom were black, stepped down from the coach and moved over to the side of the road with their hands held high. The door opened and a well-dressed man got out. His trousers were of a mustard color, his jacket lime green. He had on a brown silk vest and a white ascot. Wiping a silk handkerchief over his face, he looked at the scene. His eyes reflected some fear, but mostly anger and incredulity, as if unable to believe that someone would have the audacity to actually do this to him.

"See here, do you know who I am?" he asked importantly.

"Can't say as I do."

"I am Percy Chester, the civilian administrator to the military governor of the Hempstead military district," he said with a distinguished air.

"Would that be Yankee governor or Confederate governor?" Hank asked.

"Union, of course, seeing as the war is over," Chester said.

"You sayin' the war's over?" Bob asked.

"I most certainly am. It came across the wires yesterday. Lee surrendered at Appomattox, Virginia. The South is defeated."

"You believe that?" Hank asked Marcus.

Marcus rubbed his chin. "Yep, but it don't change much for us right now. Beauford," Marcus said, using the name to refer to Loomis, "how 'bout you climb up on top an' see what our friend the Yankee administrator is carryin'. Oh and you, Mr. Administrator, empty your pockets."

"What?" Chester sputtered. "I don't believe this! You are actually robbing me?"

"You sure are sharp for a Yankee. Now turn 'em out."

"Nothin' up here but a bag of duds like them he's wearin'," Loomis called down from the top of the coach.

"Throw it down," Hank called, who had already untied the horse and climbed aboard. He smiled at Chester. "He's about my size. Be good to wear a decent suit again."

"That's my horse," Chester sputtered.

"Mine now," Hank said easily.

"And my clothes," Chester added, seeing the bag come down from atop the coach.

"Well, you don't want me to ride a fine animal like this without the fine clothes for it, do you?" Hank asked. The boys laughed.

Marcus looked through the man's billfold, then let out a soft whistle.

"You've got over six hundred dollars in here."

"Greenbacks?" Hank asked.

"Certainly they are greenbacks," Chester answered as if insulted. "Do you think I'd have Confederate money?"

"No, but lots of people been carrying bank scrip," Hank explained, "and that's harder'n hell to get rid of."

"What are you doing with so much money?" Marcus asked.

"Well, one does find business opportunities when an area has undergone economic stress," Chester said. "I suspect there might be some land available to buy if one has the cash."

"You mean steal by payin' back taxes, don't you?" Hank said. "Jesus Christ, you're a carpetbagger. A little fancier dressed than most, but you're a carpetbagger just the same."

"Here's six hundred you won't be making deals with," Marcus said, putting the billfold in his pocket.

"What about the watch?" Billy Joe asked. "It looks like it's gold."

"No," Marcus said. "He can put out a description on the watch that might turn up on us someday.

Right now we're no different from a hundred other Confederates trying to make their way back home to Louisiana." He purposely lied about Louisiana being their home, because it was just opposite of the way they were going.

"Here's a box of Havana cigars," Loomis called triumphantly.

"Well, now. Any bourbon?"

"Sir, I'll have you know I do not drink," Chester said self-righteously.

"That a fact? Too bad, I don't trust any son of a bitch that don't drink."

"Nothing in the coach," Hank said.

"All right, let's go. Beauford, toss the box of cigars down."

"You'll pay for this," Chester sputtered. "I'll notify every military and civilian law officer in West Texas about you."

"You do that," Marcus said. "You tell them you was robbed by the Louisiana Cavaliers."

"Think we ought to tell 'em who we are?" Hank asked, holding back a grin.

"The Louisiana Cavaliers," Chester said. "I'll remember that."

"Maybe we should've picked someone else to rob. This fella seems awful smart to me," Hank went on.

Chester smiled triumphantly. "You'll rue the day you encountered Percy Chester. Mark my words, you'll rue the day."

Hank brought the other horses up to the road, and the men mounted. Marcus looked at the driver and two footmen who still had their hands up.

"Put your hands down," Marcus said. All three

men lowered their arms. "Listen, you'd better be careful through here. Gangs of outlaws been seen ridin' around, just lookin' to see who they can rob."

"Yeah," Hank said. "We was just lucky we got to you before anyone else."

Marcus pushed his men hard across West Texas, New Mexico Territory, and into Arizona Territory. They saw land the likes of which they had never seen before. They were used to trees and grass, swampland, and hilled prairies, but this was completely different. Here the land was red, brown, and open. There were no houses, fields, or even ranches to break up the vistas and the horizons were studded with red mesas and purple cliff walls. In the distance they saw blue mountains, and at night the stars and moon shed so much light that, though everything was in shades of silver and black, they could see almost as clearly as at midday.

They found themselves in the small village of Dos Cabezas. Hot and dusty, the town was little more than a two-block-long main street with fly-blown adobe buildings on either side. They stopped to stable the horses, to give them oats and a rubdown. The men bought hats, denim trousers, and cotton shirts, then paid a quarter apiece for baths at the barbershop, got a trim and shave. Cleaned up and in their new duds, they made for the only saloon for supper and a few drinks.

Supper was steak and beans, which were liberally seasoned with hot peppers, washed down with mugs of beer.

"The beans'll set you afire," Bob said. "But damn

me if they ain't about the tastiest things I've put in my mouth in quite a while." Bob smiled at one of the bar girls, and she caught his smile and returned it. Bob pushed away from the table. "Boys, I do believe I got me a little business to take care of," he said, starting toward the girl. He had a weakness for whores.

There was a pretty redhead who, though she had been "on the line" for a while as a soiled dove, had managed to retain her looks. Only her eyes gave her away. She had seen three years of men of all ages, sizes, and dispositions. Some treated her as if she were a queen, some were rude, and some were cruel. It was a risk every time she went up the stairs with a new man, though she had learned through bitter experience to be a pretty good judge of a man just on his looks. The stranger coming toward her looked like a man who would enjoy what she could do for him, pay her a fair price, and not be abusive. She might even enjoy it.

Shortly after Bob went upstairs with the bar girl, a man came into the saloon and stepped up to the bar. He stayed down at the far end where he could see the whole saloon, and he examined everyone through dark, beady eyes. He was small, wiry, and dark, with a narrow nose and thin lips. He used his left hand to hold his glass while his right hand stayed down beside the handle of his Colt .44, which was worn in such a way as to allow for a quick draw.

Only Marcus had actually noticed the man, and he studied him quietly while he ate his supper. He knew that this man was about to kill someone—knew it as clearly as if he had been dressed in a black robe, carrying a reaper, and wearing a death's mask.

The bat-wing doors swung open a moment later,

and two men came into the saloon. Both of them were wearing badges, and they stood just inside the entrance for a moment, looking around the room. One of them had eyes to match his gray hair and mustache. He was the sheriff. His deputy was much younger, and from the dark hair and eyes, Marcus guessed he might have been Mexican.

"Marcus," Loomis said nervously, touching Marcus's arm and glancing toward the two lawmen. "It's the law."

"Easy, Loomis," Marcus said quietly. "They ain't after us. They got someone else in mind."

Marcus saw the lawmen look around, then saw their gaze find the man at the bar. He saw their muscles stiffen, and when he looked at the man at the bar, he realized this was what the man had been waiting for.

"Mason," the gray sheriff said. "I got paper on you," he said. "You gonna come quiet?"

"I got no argument with you, Sheriff," the man called Mason answered, his voice high, thin, and grating. In a world without weapons he might have been a pathetic figure among men, but his long, thin fingers, delicate hands, and small, wiry body were perfectly suited for his occupation as a gunman.

"I got to take you in," the sheriff said with resignation. "Are you going to come peaceable or do I force you?"

Mason put his drink on the bar, then turned toward the sheriff. The sheriff's deputy stepped several feet to one side while still facing Mason. He bent his knees slightly and held his hand in readiness over his own pistol.

"I don't think you can force me," Mason said.

"You don't want this, Mason."

Mason smiled, but it wasn't a smile of mirth. "Well, now, Sheriff, seems like I got no choice."

Marcus saw the sheriff lick his lips nervously, then look around the room.

"Any of you fellas willin' to sign on as my deputy?"

No one volunteered. In fact, several men who considered themselves too close to any possible action got up and moved away. Only Marcus and the three with him remained at their table.

"You fellas?" the sheriff called out hopefully. "Want to earn a few dollars as my deputy?"

"Sorry, Sheriff, just ain't my business," Marcus said.

"Better listen to the man, Sheriff," Mason suggested.

Marcus watched the sheriff for a long moment. He knew exactly when the lawman was going to make his move. Marcus watched the eyes, the narrowing of the corners, the glint of the pupils, then the resignation. The sheriff started for his gun.

Mason was snake fast. By the time he had his pistol up, it was spitting a finger of flame six inches from the end of the barrel. It roared a second time, even over the shots fired by the sheriff and his deputy, and a large cloud of smoke billowed up to temporarily obscure the action. When the smoke drifted up to the ceiling a few seconds later, Mason was still standing, the smoking gun in his hand. The sheriff and his deputy were dead on the floor.

Marcus heard footsteps running upstairs, and when he saw Mason whip his gun around, Marcus drew on him. Mason heard the deadly click of sear on cylinder as the hammer came back on Marcus's gun. He looked over to see that Marcus had the drop on him.

"That's my friend up there," Marcus said quietly. "I wouldn't take too kindly to you shootin' him."

"Mister," Mason said in his narrow, grating voice, "you gonna deal yourself into this hand?"

"Put your gun away, back on out of here, and we'll call it even," Marcus said.

"Only it ain't even," Mason said. "Somebody pulls a gun on me, I gotta call 'em on it."

"Then you're gonna die."

The vein in Mason's temple throbbed for a long moment, as if he was trying to make up his mind what to do. Finally a thin smile played across his face and he slipped his pistol back into his holster.

"All right," he said. "I'll let it go this time."

"Damn big of you," Marcus said.

"We may run into each other again."

"Could be."

"I'll be lookin' forward to it," Mason said. Backing carefully across the floor, he put his hand behind him and pushed open the bat-wing doors.

Five

TIRED OF SLEEPING on the ground, the boys decided to take hotel rooms after supper. Bob and Loomis took one together, as did Hank and Billy Joe. Marcus got a room of his own. The hotel rooms taken care of, Hank and Loomis returned to the saloon to find a card game. Bob surrounded himself with the bar girls, and Billy Joe decided to have a second supper. That left Marcus alone, so he decided to take a walk around the town.

It was dark now, and the street was lighted only by spills of yellow from the open doors and windows of the saloons and cantinas. High overhead, the stars winked brightly, while over a distant mesa the moon hung like a large silver wheel. He could hear music, the thrum of guitars, a lilting song in a language he couldn't understand, and from somewhere the single, clarion sound of a trumpet.

Until the last several weeks, Marcus had not been around Mexicans much. There were Mexicans in Texas, though until recently, most of his experience had been in East Texas where there were fewer. They seemed a happy enough lot, he thought, and they sung about as much as the Negroes back home.

When Marcus reached the end of the street, he turned and started back. Suddenly two men with knives jumped from the shadows between the buildings and attacked. He responded quickly, avoiding one blade, but catching the tip of the other in his side. One inch closer and he would have been disemboweled.

The would-be assassins were both wearing white peon shirts and trousers, so that despite the darkness of the street they were easy to see. One of them moved in to try and finish Marcus off, but Quinn dropped to the ground, twisted, and thrust his feet out, catching the attacker on the chest, driving him back several feet. The other one moved in, keeping Marcus off his feet and away from his gun.

The assailants were good: skilled and agile. But they were small, giving Marcus a little advantage. Quinn sent a booted foot whistling toward one of them, catching the man in the groin. Then he lunged upward and rammed a hard fist into the teeth of the other man. He felt the teeth loosen and crack.

"Aiiyee!" the assailant screamed, dropping his knife and reaching up to his mouth.

The other man ran to his partner, and pulling on him, broke off the fight. They ran around the corner and disappeared into the shadows before Marcus managed to get a look at them.

"Mister," a pained voice called from the shadows of a nearby building. "Help me, mister."

"Where are you?"

"Over here, on the ground."

Disregarding his own wound, Marcus moved into the shadows. There he saw a man on his hands and knees, trying to rise. Marcus helped him to his feet.

"Much obliged," the man said. "Those two jumped me an' would'a got my money belt if you hadn't come along to pull 'em off me."

Marcus chuckled dryly. "Hate to disappoint you, mister," he said. "But I didn't pull them off you. They jumped me."

"They must'a thought you was comin' to my rescue," the man said. "It all comes out the same. Could you . . . could you help me back to the hotel?"

"All right," Marcus said, taking the man's arms around his shoulder and walking with him for support.

"The name's Harbin. Jim Harbin," the wounded man said. "I'm foreman for the Double X, down in Diablo. You heard of it?"

"Can't say as I have."

"One of the biggest spreads in the territory. Owned by a fella named Ike Elam. Listen, if you're lookin' for work, Mr. Elam lets me purt' near do all the hirin' and firin'. I'd be glad to sign you on."

"I don't know," Marcus said. "I never worked a ranch . . . not sure I could."

"What do you do?"

"Well, last five years I been killin' people," Marcus said dryly.

"The war?"

Marcus nodded.

"Mister, I hate to admit it, but I reckon that talent is worth as much punchin' cows in these parts. If you're lookin' for work with your guns, you'll find that soon enough."

By the time they reached the hotel, Harbin was able to stand on his own two feet. He walked unsteadily through the door and into the hotel lobby. Marcus went with him.

"I'm all right now," Harbin said. "Thanks."

"Glad I could oblige."

"Father!" a woman's voice called, and Marcus looked around to see a beautiful young woman standing halfway down the stairs. She was tall and slender with blond hair and blue eyes. She hurried across the lobby to her father. "What happened? Are you all right?"

"I'm fine," Harbin said. "Thanks to this gentleman," he added, pointing to Marcus. "Two Mex's jumped me, intent on cuttin' my throat and robbin' me, I suppose. But this fella come along and run them off. Mr. Quinn, this is my daughter, Julie."

"What a brave thing to do," the woman said.

"Look, don't get the wrong idea, ma'am," Marcus said. "I was just walkin' down there polite as you please. They jumped me before I even saw them."

"And yet you still beat them off? That's all the more reason to—oh, you're hurt!"

Marcus didn't realize it, but he made quite a sight. He was holding his hand over his belly wound, but the blood was seeping around his fingers. The new cotton shirt and denim trousers he had just bought were soaked with blood.

"Where are you staying? Do you have a room?"

"Yes, ma'am," Marcus said. He waved his hand and the blood shined red in the soft light of the hotel lobby. "Right here," he added.

"Go up to your room quickly," she said. "What number is it? I'll come tend to your wound."

"Number twelve," Marcus said. He grabbed his belly wound again. "Might be good to lie down at that."

As Marcus started up the stairs, he discovered that the wound was bothering him more than he first thought. He had to stop halfway up and lean against the wall to get his breath. When he went on, he left a stain of blood on the wall.

Once inside his room, he ripped the bed sheet in two and wrapped it around his side, pressing it tightly against his wound. When the crude bandage was in place, he lay on the bed, closed his eyes, and fell asleep.

Marcus opened his eyes. Something had awakened him and he lay very still. The doorknob turned, and Marcus was up, reaching for the gun that lay on the table by his bed.

He moved as quickly as a cat, forgetting the wound in his stomach. But the wound didn't let him forget, and he sucked in a gasp of air through clenched teeth as a bolt of pain shot through him.

Moving despite the pain, Marcus stepped to the side of the door, cocking his Colt .44. Naked from the waist up, he felt the night air on his skin. His senses were alert, his body alive with readiness.

Marcus could hear someone breathing on the

other side of the door. A thin shaft of hall light shot underneath. From somewhere in the night, a guitar played and someone laughed. He wondered where his men were—what they were doing? Suddenly he smiled as he recalled the girl's promise to come tend to his wound. He took a deep breath and smelled the scent of lilacs, the same scent he had noticed earlier.

"Miss Harbin?" he called.

"Are you awake?" Julie called back.

Marcus eased the hammer down on the pistol, then opened the door to let a wide bar of light spill into the room. The hall lantern was backlighting the thin, cotton dress the girl was wearing, and he could see her body in shadow behind the cloth. It had been a time since he had had a woman, and he felt an ache that transcended the pain of the knife cut.

"Come on in," Marcus invited, stepping back to let her step inside. He lit the candle on his table and a bubble of light illuminated the room.

"I . . . uh . . . don't know your name," Julie stammered.

"Quinn. Marcus Quinn."

Julie held up some bandages and a jar of salve. "I came to tend to your wound if you'll let me."

"All right," Marcus agreed. He took away the bandage he had made from the bed sheet, then lay back on his bed and loosened his belt. He slid his trousers down a few inches, exposing the entire length of the wound, but at the same time showing the top of a thick bush of pubic hair.

"Oh, I, uh . . ." Julie turned her head away in shame, but even as she did so, Marcus noticed that she sucked in a quick gasp of air. He had seen that reaction in women before and he knew what it meant.

"How does it look?" Marcus asked.

"I don't know." Julie was still looking away.

"Can't know without looking," Marcus said. He took her arm and pulled her down so that she was sitting on the bed beside him, then he put his hand to her face and turned it toward him, feeling the heat in her skin. She looked at his wound, at his flat stomach, then she gently reached out and touched him. Her fingers felt cool.

"I, uh, had better clean it," she said. She walked over to the chifferobe where a basin and a pitcher of water stood. She poured water into the basin, then brought it back to the bed and began gently bathing his stomach. Within a few minutes she had washed away all the dried blood and was now looking at the cut. It was thin and clean.

"What do you think?" Marcus asked.

She put her hand back on his stomach lightly and left it there. The feel of it set Marcus's blood boiling. "The wound is really not that bad," she said. "The bleeding has stopped and it's clean. A little salve is all it needs."

"Yeah," Marcus said. "But that isn't all I need."

"What . . . what do you mean?"

"You're a growed woman, Julie Harbin. I been around enough women to know what you're thinking about that right now."

"Oh . . . I assure you, sir, you're wrong," Julie stammered.

"Am I?"

"Yes," Julie insisted.

Marcus let go of her arm. "All right, if I'm wrong, get up and walk on out of this room."

Julie sat there for a long moment, neither moving nor speaking.

"Well?" Marcus asked.

"I . . . I find myself quite unable to move," Julie said in a quiet, frightened voice. It was obvious to Marcus that she was more frightened of herself than she was of him.

Marcus reached up to touch her again, and he let his hand rest lightly on her neck. "Maybe you never had a man and wonderin' what it's like. Or maybe you remember how good it was and you want to do it again, only a proper lady ain't supposed to just 'cause she got the hankerin'."

"Please," Julie said, her breath coming in short gasps. "You mustn't talk like this."

"Why not? I always been a man who talked straight. We ain't ever seen each other before, probably never see each other again. Makes it simple."

Julie didn't take her hand away from his skin. Instead, she moved it back and forth, gently stroking him, even letting her fingers dip daringly into the hair. Marcus unbuttoned his trousers and then slid his pants the rest of the way down. By now he was totally erect and when it sprang up, she reacted in an audible gasp.

Marcus put his hand up behind her head and pulled her mouth down to his. He kissed her lightly at first, then harder as he felt her hand move boldly to the shaft of his penis.

Marcus began to undo the buttons of her dress. With her free hand she helped unfasten the bodice.

The combination of light from the dim candle and the silver moon played across her flesh, disclosing small breasts and nipples, pink and erect with desire.

Julie slipped the garment from her body, then stood naked in the soft light. Her smooth flesh gleamed. Her legs were shapely and strong, and met at a luxurious growth of blond hair. He held his arms out to her and she went to him, kissing him deeply, pressing her naked flesh against his, pushing her hard little nipples into his chest. Her fingernails raked down his back, across his buttocks, onto his scrotum.

Marcus moved lower with his mouth, along her jawline to her ear, where he made her gasp by sticking his tongue inside it. He trailed his tongue down her throat to her shoulder, then down across the soft, smooth flesh of her breast to touch it to the nipple. He took it between his teeth gently and began to suck.

"Oh, you were right," Julie said. "This is what I wanted." Her hand grasped his cock, squeezed it, then worked up and down the shaft.

She kissed his forehead, then his hair. A moment later she was on the bed beside him, then under him, offering herself to him.

With a quick, smooth movement, Marcus was over her. She guided him into her.

Marcus withheld his thrust for a moment to kiss her again. Then he stuck his tongue into her mouth at the same time he pushed himself into her velvet cleft. She let out a little whimper, but thrust her hips up as hard as she could, taking him into her hot, pulsing tunnel.

She flailed about wildly beneath him, gyrating her

hips, forcing him to stay with her, to ride her like a bucking bronco. He thrust all the way in, then pulled out, then rammed it home again while she squeezed him with tiny, but intense muscle spasms.

"Oh . . . oh . . . I feel so . . ." she said as the familiar feelings began approaching a crescendo. Then she cried out in sharp little moans as she crashed over the peak of her first orgasm, then moved quickly in search of another. Lightning struck her a second time, then a third, and she shuddered with the pleasure of it.

Marcus stayed with her. The fire in her body spread to his and he felt the sweet-hot boiling of his own blood and sperm as he shot his seed deep into her womb.

Outside, in the darkness of the town, Marcus heard a rider pass, his horse's hoofbeats ringing hollowly on the quiet street. From a nearby saloon he heard a man's low, rumbling voice, followed by the laughter of several patrons, a woman's high-pitched trill being the most discernible. On the prairie he heard a coyote howl.

"Oh," Julie said quietly. "Oh, my, what you must think of me."

"I think you're quite a lady," Marcus said.

"You must believe me . . . I've never done anything like this before."

"I know."

"I'm telling the truth. I've never—"

"It don't matter," Marcus said, interrupting her gently. "Remember?"

"Oh . . . oh, yes, I suppose you're right," she said.

She had been lying beside him, but she got up now and walked over to the window to look out onto the street. He could see her clearly in the soft, golden light of the single candle and the silver glow of the moon. Her breasts were in bold relief, her nipples erect, but the lower part of her body was shrouded in shadow. She pulled the curtain to one side and looked out.

"See anything out there?" Marcus asked.

She looked back at him and smiled. "No, not really," she said. She turned toward him. "I guess you'll be gone tomorrow."

"I reckon I will," Marcus agreed with a quiet chuckle, "but we still have the rest of the night."

Six

ONE HUNDRED MILES south of where Marcus lay at this moment was the tiny town of Diablo, Arizona Territory. Diablo was significant only because it was the first settlement on the American side of the Mexican border. Diablo existed to serve the two large ranches which lay nearby. One was Ike Elam's Double X Ranch. Ike had bought cotton cheap just before the war. After the war began he had the cotton ginned and milled into broadcloth. He sold the cloth to the United States Army for four times what it was actually worth. Then, with money in hand, he moved to Arizona to be as far from the war as he could and filed for the ranch land under the Homestead Act. The fact that he had filed under twenty different names, then "bought" the homestead parcels from each of the phony names didn't matter. What did matter was that he controlled nearly half of all the land in the Silver River Valley.

The rest of the land was owned by Don Juan de la Montoya. He was a citizen of the United States by virtue of the fact that all of Arizona had been ceded to the United States. Although he was an American citizen, he and his family were no less Mexican, and followed Spanish customs of the old ways. Because of that, his younger brother, Esteban, traveled from his home in Buenaventura to visit Juan and secure his brother's blessings on his upcoming marriage. Esteban brought several of his servants, his bride-to-be, seventeen-year-old Carlotta Sanchez, and her servants with him.

In most of the towns along the Arizona and Mexico border, the Americans and the Mexicans got along well. But in Diablo there was tension. Ike Elam claimed that several sections of untitled land were his by right of possession. Juan Montoya was just as vehement that the land was his by right of the Spanish Land Grant, a legal tenet that had been recognized by the United States courts.

The dispute had gotten out of hand a few times—a line shack was burned, some cattle were run away from water, a cowboy from the Double X was stripped naked and set afoot, and one of Montoya's men was badly beaten up. So far there had been no shooting but everyone agreed that gunplay was the next step.

In the town of Diablo, two dozen adobe buildings lay around a dusty plaza, baking under the hot Arizona sun. Fully one-quarter of the buildings in town were drinking establishments, called cantinas by the Mexicans, saloons by the Americans.

Ike Elam's men frequented the New York Saloon when they were in town. Although the outside of the New York looked like every other building in Diablo, the owner made every effort to try and make it look as un-Mexican as it possibly could inside. The focal point of everyone who entered the New York Saloon was the large painting of a New York street scene, which hung behind the bar. The saloon served only beer and bourbon. A sign on the wall read:

ANYONE WHO ORDERS
TEQUILA
WILL BE PUT OUT OF
THIS ESTABLISHMENT.

The New York Saloon was the only place in town that had a piano, and it was grinding away as a handful of Double X men sat around a table.

"They say this Esteban Montoya is real good with a gun. They say he run off Pancho Juárez near 'bout single-handed," Curly said.

"He come here to get his brother's say-so to get married. He even brought the girl with him. She's a purty thing. I seen her an' her family last Sunday mornin' when they come into town to go to church."

"You was in church, Deekus?" Shorty asked with a laugh.

"No, I was just headin' back to the ranch from a night of drinkin'." Everyone around the table laughed.

"He's a grown man, ain't he? Why's he have to ask his brother?"

"That's just the way them Mex's do things," Shorty explained.

"Yeah, well, married or not, I don't like Montoya gettin' a gunsel from down in Mexico. We ain't got no one can match up with him."

"Well, I figure that's been took care of," Deekus said.

"How?"

"Elam sent Harbin up to Dos Cabezas to hire a few more hands. If it's gonna come to a shoot out, he don't aim for us to be caught a day late an' a dollar short when it comes to havin' fightin' men."

"You think Harbin'll be able to find anybody?" Shorty asked.

"I hear tell Mr. Elam give him five hundred dollars in cash to take with him. He damn well better find somebody," Deekus said, and the others laughed.

"I thought I seen him an' his daughter leavin' on the stage yesterday," Curly said.

"Why'd his daughter go along with him?"

"She went up to buy some school books for the school she's runnin'."

"You ask me, we ought to close down that school," Curly said. "There's too many Mexicans in it."

Deekus nodded. "But I reckon that's good. Them little Mex kids is likely get to talkin' about things and the Harbin girl might pick up somethin' we can use."

"You think she'll tell her pa?" Shorty asked.

"I reckon if it's serious enough, she'd pass it on to him, an' he'd tell us."

"You think Harbin'll tell us?" Curly asked.

"You think he won't?"

"Can't never tell about him. He got a peculiar idea about right an' wrong," Curly said. "Iffen he thinks we're in the right, he'll do everythin' he can to help out. But iffen he don't, he likely won't do nothin' at all."

"He's Ike Elam's foreman," Deekus said. "I figure he'll do exactly what Mr. Elam tells him or he won't be keepin' his job."

Don Juan de la Montoya was fifty-four years old; his brother Esteban was forty-three. Juan had married late in life, but was now enjoying the fruits of a family. He had a beautiful wife and four children, from five to thirteen years of age. Esteban had never been married before but was about to take a bride who was many years younger than he. That was not unusual in the Montoya family.

Family tradition was not the only reason Esteban was in Diablo. His brother would need his help if the range war everyone talked about really did begin. Esteban, a provisional colonel in the Mexican Federal Reserve, had recently been involved in a confrontation with the Sonora Banditos. He had fought with such honor that he was awarded a medal by the Mexican government.

Juan and his younger brother Esteban had just ridden to the top of a rocky mesa. From this vantage point they could see thousands of acres of Montoya land. Most of the land was dry, baked brown under the relentless summer sun. However, a long thin line of green snaked its way across the valley floor. The green was the vegetation that grew alongside the

Silver River, where the cattle congregated both for water and food. Because of the scarcity of grass and water, it required three times as many acres to support cattle here. That was why the ranches had to be so large.

"Now that you have seen all the ranch, my brother, what do you think of it?" Juan asked.

"I think it is *magnifico*," Esteban said enthusiastically. "I think it may be the—uhn!" Esteban suddenly put his hand to his chest. When he pulled it away, it was smeared with blood. "Juan?" he asked in a pained, questioning voice.

Neither man had heard the first shot, and thus the rifle bullet that buried itself deep in Esteban's chest was a surprise. Juan heard the second shot, not only the report of the rifle, but the little thudding sound it made when it, too, hit Esteban. Esteban reeled for a second, then tumbled out of his saddle. Juan pulled out his own rifle, then leaped from his saddle and knelt beside his brother. He waved his sombrero at the horses, sending them out of the line of fire.

"Let that be a lesson to you, Mex! Stay off Double X land!" someone called. Juan looked toward the sound of the voice, but he could see no one. Then he looked down at his brother and saw that Esteban's eyes were open and vacant.

"Esteban!" Juan shouted in pain. He put his hand on his brother's shoulder and shook him, but he got no response. Then, sadly, he reached up to close Esteban's eyes. His brother was dead.

As great as Juan's sorrow over his brother's death was his anger and thirst for revenge. He ran to the back of the mesa and saw three men riding toward the Double X Ranch.

"Elam," Montoya said aloud as he spat in the dirt.

They were out of rifle range, but he still raised his rifle and fired at them.

There were three cowboys inside the small adobe line shack. One was asleep on the bunk; the other two were sitting across a barrel head from each other, playing cards. They were playing for matches only, but that didn't lessen the intensity of their game. When one of them with a pair of aces took the pot, the other one complained.

"You son of a bitch! Where did you get that ace?" His oath was softened by a burst of laughter.

"Don't you know? I took it from Shorty's boot when he was asleep."

"Does Shorty keep an ace in his boot?"

"You think he don't? I never know'd him to do anythin' honest when he could cheat."

"That's the truth. But Deekus is just as bad."

"So's Curly."

The cards were raked in, the deck shuffled, then redealt.

"You think Shorty's the one shot that Mexican?" the dealer asked.

"Yep, I do. But when I said somethin' to Elam about it, look what it got me. I'm out here doin' line shack duty."

"I just don't get Elam. It's almost like he wanted this here range war. Last week one of Montoya's riders brought back four of our cows that had strayed over onto their land. I thought it was real neighborly, but Elam said I should' a shot 'im. He said havin' the cows with him was all the proof we needed they'd been stole."

The cowboy on the bunk spoke for the first time.

"Seems to me like you boys should know by now to keep your mouths shut. Whatever Elam's doin' don't got nothin' to do with us."

"Maybe not," the dealer replied. "But I don't much like workin' for someone that'd shoot a man down for no reason a'tall."

Four riders wearing sombreros and serapes stopped on a little hill overlooking a Double X line shack, then ground-tied their mounts about thirty yards behind them. They moved to the edge of the hill at a crouch, then looked down toward the little adobe building.

The leader gave the signal and all four men raised their rifles.

"Shoot," the leader said, squeezing the trigger that sent out the first bullet.

The dealer died instantly, a bullet coming through the window to crash into the back of his head. His partner went next, a bullet in his chest. The cowboy on the bunk rolled onto the floor.

"Jesus!" he said. "It's the Mexicans!"

The shooting continued for another full minute, then the riders rode off into the night.

"Billy!" the wounded man on the floor called. "Billy, I'm hit bad."

Billy crawled over to the wounded man, then saw the blood on his chest. The wound was sucking air and Billy knew it would be over shortly. He put his hand on the wounded man's forehead.

"I'll get 'em for you, Jake. I promise you that," he said. "I'll get them Mexican bastards for this."

When the riders were far enough away from the line shack, the leader held up his hand and they stopped. He reached into his saddlebag and took out a bottle, then pulled the cork. He took a couple of swallows, then wiped the back of his hand across his mouth and handed it to the rider nearest him.

"You think the gringo will be pleased, José?" asked the man as he took the bottle.

"*Si*," the leader said and passed the tequila to the next man. "He will pay *mucho*."

Seven

WHEN MARCUS SHOWED up for breakfast the next morning, the others made room for him around their table, then continued their discussion of the previous night. Bob had been absent, having spent the night with a girl he'd picked up in the bar. Marcus had his own diversion with Julie. Hank, Billy Joe, and Loomis had spent the night gambling, drinking, and, in Hank's words, "raisin' hell."

"You missed a good time," Loomis said.

Hank looked at Marcus and smiled. "I'm not so sure about that," he said. "I don't know but what he might have had a better time."

"He could'a had as good a time as me," Bob said. "But there's no way it could'a been better."

Everyone laughed at Bob's declaration, then looked up as a man approached their breakfast table.

"Boys, this is Jim Harbin," Marcus said. "I met him last night."

"And," Harbin said, "lucky for me." He nodded at the others by way of greeting.

"How's that?" Hank asked.

"A couple of Mexicans were fixin' to jump him. When I come by, they jumped me instead. I fought them off. Got a belly wound to show for it."

"It sure saved my neck," Harbin said. "Do you gents mind if I join you? I have a proposition you might find interestin' and profitable."

"Get the man a chair, Loomis," Marcus ordered. Loomis moved a chair from a nearby table and Harbin sat down. He dropped a yellow piece of paper on the table in front of him.

"This here is a telegram I just got from my boss, Ike Elam. Like I told you last night, Quinn, Elam owns a ranch, the Double X, about one hundred miles south of here, near the town of Diablo. He's authorized me to hire five or six good men."

"Harbin, I told you we ain't ranch hands," Marcus said.

"Yes, sir. Billy Joe there has ate more cows than any of us ever punched," Bob added, poking fun at Billy Joe's appetite.

"Oh, this ain't about workin' the herd, boys," Harbin said, waving the suggestion away with his hand. "I want you to do what I know you're good at—fightin' a war."

Marcus and his men looked at each other for a moment, then Marcus spoke.

"Mister, we just come through one war. What

makes you think we'd be interested in gettin' into another one?"

"This war ain't nothin' like the one you just come through. And it ain't for no army pay, neither."

"We're listening," Hank said.

Harbin sat back and told Marcus and the others about the range war between Elam and Montoya. He told them about the latest killings on both sides. "So now this war's on," he concluded. "And the job's yours if you'll take it."

"What's the pay?" Marcus asked.

"One hundred dollars a man and found," Harbin said. "I'll give you half your pay now, the other half after you been there for a week."

Marcus leaned back in his chair and folded his arms across his chest. They had taken six hundred dollars from Percy Chester, but at least half of that was gone. One hundred dollars apiece was five hundred dollars with free food and board. He looked at the others.

"Anybody object to this?" he asked.

"It's as good as anything we got going," Hank said.

"Be fun," Loomis suggested.

"Fine by me," Bob agreed.

"I'm in," Billy Joe added. "Loomis, you goin' to eat them biscuits?"

Without a word Loomis slid the biscuits toward Billy Joe.

"All right, Mr. Harbin," Marcus said. "It looks like you've hired yourself the finest small fighting unit in the South."

* * *

"If you have no objections, señorita," Juan said, "I will bury my brother here on Rancho Montoya. It is where I wish to be buried and where my family will be buried. He will be with his loved ones."

"Señor, it is not my place to say where he should be buried," Carlotta replied, surprised that she had been consulted.

"But it is. In another day you would have been his widow and the decision of his final resting place would have been yours."

"Then I say let us bury him here," Carlotta said. "I am sure he will rest happily, knowing he has the love of his brother and his brother's family to watch over him."

"Thank you, Carlotta, you are most gracious," Juan said. He nodded to his foreman who left quietly to prepare the grave in the family cemetery where one of Juan's children and the father and mother of his wife already lay buried.

Although it was a small funeral, it was conducted with great dignity, and in addition to everyone from the ranch, nearly all the Mexicans and a dozen or so Americans came out from the town and the surrounding ranches. Padre Delgado of the local mission church conducted the service.

When Carlotta Sanchez, still dressed in funeral black, returned from the burial of her fiancé, she went into the small family chapel just off the main living room and lit a candle for his soul. Then she knelt in front of the altar and prayed very hard, not only for Esteban's soul but for her own, because she believed that his getting killed was her fault.

Her marriage had been arranged by Carlotta's

father. Her father knew that such a marriage was a wonderful match, because Don Esteban de la Montoya was not only a member of the wealthy Montoya family, he was the owner of a large ranch in northern Mexico. He was also a well-known local hero who had fought and defeated the Sonora Banditos.

But Esteban was forty-three years old and Carlotta was only seventeen. If she married someone that old, she would become an old woman before her time. She had prayed during the long journey up to Rancho Montoya for something to prevent the marriage.

Now there would be no wedding because Esteban was dead, and Carlotta was certain she was the cause of it.

By the time Carlotta finished with her prayers, she knew that she must do. She would stay with Juan and his family and be the sister to them that she would have been had she married Esteban. And she would never marry, but remain true to Esteban's memory for as long as she lived. It was a penance she owed for the sin she had committed.

"But, of course, we would be happy to have you stay with us," Miguelina said when Carlotta told her of her plans. "Juan, see how sweet she is?"

"Yes," Juan agreed. He kept to himself any worry about the range war he knew was about to erupt. In fact, he had thought of sending Miguelina and their children and Carlotta back to Mexico. The only reason he did not was because he was afraid that they would be subjected to a greater danger during the trip back.

"I have an idea," Miguelina suggested. "We can send Carlotta and the children to the school in Diablo. Miss Harbin is a wonderful teacher and Carlotta can learn much from her."

"Yes," Juan agreed. "That is a good idea." Miss Harbin, he knew, was the daughter of the foreman of the Double X Ranch. He was certain that the school would be a safe haven, no matter how ferocious the fighting became.

Carlotta was equally happy about the decision. She very much wanted to finish her education, and by helping to watch over the Montoya children, she believed she would be paying the debt of honor she owed the Montoya family.

Pedro Bustamante raised the binoculars to his eyes and looked down toward the little camp. There were two wagons and four men in the camp. Pedro was certain there would be something valuable inside the wagons.

Pedro had bandoleers of rifle ammunition that crisscrossed his chest, a pistol belt full of cartridges around his waist, and a long knife in a scabbard that hung down his back, just behind his shoulder. He was wearing a large sombrero and a full beard. He lowered the binoculars and looked around at the men who were waiting in a small draw behind him. They, like him, were wearing criss-crossed bandoleers. There were nine, including himself, who came across the border when they got word that a range war was brewing between a big gringo rancher and Juan Montoya.

Pedro Bustamante had no love for Montoya, and he

hated gringos. He came across the border in pursuit of opportunity. He could attack both sides with impunity, take whatever spoils there were to take, and get back across the border before anyone was the wiser.

Bustamante held up four fingers indicating how many men were with the wagons. He waved his men after him, and they started toward the little camp.

Quinn and the others were quite a distance away when they heard the gunfire. They had no idea what the shooting was about, but they had come to join a war and figured this might be part of it.

"Let's go," Marcus said.

"When we get there, which side do we fight on?" Hank asked as they spurred their horses into a gallop.

"We figure that out later," Marcus replied.

"Hell," Bob said and laughed. "Let's just take on whoever's left."

It took them four minutes of hard riding to reach the scene. When they crested a little hill and looked down below them, they saw four bodies on the ground and two wagons being looted. The men who were helping themselves to the contents of the wagons were Mexican.

"Looks like you called it right, Bob," Marcus said. "We'll take on who's left. Let's get them."

Quinn's Raiders had done the same thing many times during the war—bursting onto a scene of battle totally unexpected. They had learned that such complete surprise could overcome phenomenal odds, much greater than the odds that faced them now.

Quinn's Raiders

Quinn's first shot took one of the Mexicans out of his saddle before he even knew he was in danger. Billy Joe, firing the Mare's Leg, hit the corner of one of the wagons and chewed off a large chunk of wood. Loomis dropped another Mexican and Bob got a third. Hank was carrying a shotgun and wasn't yet in range.

The Mexicans returned fire, and Quinn heard a bullet cut the air as it whistled by him. He leaned over the neck of his horse and continued the charge. He hit one of the Mexicans in the knee and heard him cry out with pain. Hank cut loose with his shotgun, peppering one of the Mexicans and the flank of his horse with buckshot. Bob had his hat shot from his head and the bullet spooked his horse. He kept his saddle and still managed to return fire. The remaining Mexicans, seeing they were no match for the crazy Americans, urged their horses into a gallop, abandoning the spoils. Marcus halted his men at the wagons, and though they fired a few parting shots at the bandits, they didn't go after them.

Loomis was the first to dismount and look at the eight men lying in the dirt.

"What is in the wagons?" Marcus asked.

Bob looked through the load, pushing a few items around to get a better look.

"Looks like some cloth, washboards, shoe black, and something called Extract of Buchu Elixer, whatever the hell that is," Hank said.

"Anything we can use?"

"Apple peelers, ladies' corsets, picture frames," Hank went on, reading the labels from the boxes.

Marcus sighed and ran his hand through his hair. "Eight men died for a couple of cases of corsets?" he asked digustedly.

"Looks like."

"All right, throw the bodies in the back of the wagons and we'll take them into town."

"Damn," Hank said. "You'd think that with two wagons there'd be something worth taking."

Ike Elam was in town to meet the afternoon stage. His foreman, Jim Harbin, and Harbin's daughter, Julie, were on the stage. Ike wanted to know if Harbin had been successful in hiring any more guns.

On his own he had hired a man named Mason the day before. This morning Mason had ridden into town with Elam and his wife, Lucy.

Lucy Elam was quite a bit younger than Ike. She was a beautiful, dark-haired, full-busted woman who had married Ike three years ago when he came up to San Francisco on a business trip.

Although she never told Ike, Lucy had come to San Francisco under the cloud of scandal, having been the mistress of a precinct police captain in New York City a few months earlier. She left New York when she got caught up in a scandal that threatened not only the police captain, but the mayor and a couple of congressmen. She was given passage on a clipper ship to San Francisco and enough money to keep her quiet.

But marrying Ike Elam had been a disaster for a woman like Lucy. He was more interested in his ranch than sex. No matter what she did, she couldn't change him. One afternoon when she tried to get him interested by walking naked in front of him, he got angry and told her to cover herself at once. "You're acting like a harlot," he told her.

"I once heard that a woman should occasionally act the harlot for her husband," Lucy said.

"That's bull. A woman should always be decent in front of her husband, excepting at night when he can't hardly see her at all."

After three long years in Diablo, Lucy was ready for a change.

Ike got down from the buckboard and moved out into the street to meet the coach as it arrived.

"Good to see you back, Harbin," Ike said as his foreman stepped down from the coach. "What happened to you?" he asked when he noticed the bruises on Harbin's face.

"Got jumped by a couple of galoots," he said.

"Did they get the money?"

"Mr. Elam, my father could have been killed," Julie said, alighting behind her father, "and all you're concerned with is whether they got the money."

"No, of course I'm concerned for your father as well," Ike said. "But I can see that he's all right."

"They didn't get the money," Harbins' said. "I gave that to the five men I hired to come down here."

"We'll need 'em," Elam said. "That is, if they show up."

"Oh, they'll come," Harbin said. "I only gave them half the money. I think they'll want the other half."

"Yeah, well, the question is, are they good enough men for the job?"

"I know the leader is," Harbin said. "He's a fella named Marcus Quinn, and he's the one saved my hide when those two varmints tried to cut my throat."

Upon hearing Marcus's name, Julie gasped and put her hand to her mouth.

"What is it, girl?" Harbin asked his daughter. "Something wrong?"

"Did you . . . did you say you hired Mr. Quinn to come here?"

"Yes, the next day," Harbin said. "I saw him leave the hotel and go across the street to breakfast. I followed him and saw that there were four others with him. Hired 'em on the spot."

"Oh," Julie said. Her face flushed and she walked to the back of the coach, then stood there for a few moments with her hand resting on the wheel. Her father started talking with Ike Elam and paid no attention to his daughter. Lucy noticed, however, and she got down from the buckboard and went over to talk to the younger woman.

"Are you all right?" Lucy asked.

"Yes," Julie answered. "Yes, I'm fine. The coach . . . it was close and it's a hot day. I just needed a little air, that's all."

"Of course," Lucy said. "I'm sure that's it."

Lucy was sure that wasn't it, but she had no idea what else could be bothering Julie.

"Julie, don't go off without your luggage," her father called.

"I'll get your luggage, miss," Mason said, swinging down from his horse and starting for the stage.

"Thank you," Julie said.

"You can put it in the buckboard," Lucy told him. "Julie, why don't you come with me into the emporium? We'll have a glass of lemonade."

"Yes, thank you," Julie said. "A glass of lemonade would be good."

Mason put the girl's carpetbag in the buckboard, then looked up so see her through the window of the emporium and saw the Elam woman and the Harbin girl sitting at a table sipping lemonade. He had never seen anyone more beautiful than Julie Harbin, and right then and there he was determined to have her.

And no man had better stand in his way.

Eight

WHEN THE TWO wagons pulled into town, it got everyone's attention. Bob drove the first wagon, Billy Joe the second. Marcus, Hank, and Loomis rode alongside, leading two empty horses.

"Who are those men?" someone asked.

"Don't know. What are they doin' with Varner's wagons?"

A twelve-year-old barefoot boy, his shirt flapping out of his trousers, ran out into the street and trotted alongside the wagon. He saw the bodies inside, then shouted the news to the entire town.

"It's Mr. Varner!" the boy said. "He's dead an' so's all the others. They's four . . ." he said before looking back into the second wagon and seeing the bodies of the Mexicans. "No, they's seven . . . eight dead men in these wagons. Four American an' four Mex."

"Did you kill Varner, mister?" someone asked

Marcus. Marcus and the others stared straight ahead.

From the stores, saloons, cantinas, barbershops, and cafes, Diablo citizens, alerted by the boy's words and the shouts of others, came outside to move silently down the street, keeping pace alongside the wagons. Finally the wagons reached the center of the plaza, where Billy Joe and Bob set the brakes, then climbed down.

The sheriff came out into the plaza, looked at the eight corpses, then took off his hat and wiped his forehead with a dirty red bandanna.

"Who're they, Sheriff?" someone asked, pointing to the Mexicans.

"I don't recognize them," the sheriff said. He looked toward the group of brown-skinned citizens who, forming half the population of Diablo, had turned out with equal interest. "Any of you know them?"

There was silence among the Mexicans, then one of them spoke hesitantly.

"That one is Manuel," he said, pointing to one of the bodies. "He's my cousin."

"He live here in Diablo, Jesus? I never seen him before."

"He live in Mexico," Jesus said. "He's a bad man . . . he rides with Pedro Bustamante."

At the mention of Bustamante's name, everyone buzzed with excitement. They had all heard of Pedro Bustamante. The bandit had built quite a reputation for himself south of the border, robbing banks, raiding entire villages, fighting pitched battles with the Federales.

"I never heard of Bustamante on this side of the border," the sheriff said. He looked at Quinn and the others. "Who're you fellas?" he asked. "How'd you get involved in this?"

"They work for the Double X," Harbin said, speaking up quickly. "Glad to see you men made it. Had some trouble, I see."

"Not much," Marcus said. "We heard some shooting so we had a look-see. When we saw eight or nine of these Mexican bandits around these two wagons, we moved. These men were already dead," he added, pointing to the Americans. "We killed these four."

"Five of you against nine of Bustamante's men?"

"Your numbers are right, mister," Marcus said.

"Well, that's Ed Varner," the sheriff said, pointing to one of the bodies. "He owns these wagons, runs freight in and out of town."

"You mean he used to run freight in and out of town," Elam said. He stepped up to Marcus and stuck his paw out toward him. "I'm Ike Elam. I own the Double X."

"You men cowhands, are you?" the sheriff asked. He asked the question in a tone of voice that made it obvious that he didn't think they were cowhands.

"Not 'xactly," Marcus said without going into any further detail.

"More guns, Elam?" the sheriff asked. The sheriff knew about Mason.

"A man's got a right to protect his property, Sheriff," Elam said. "You heard what the Mex's did to my men the other night. Kilt two of 'em while they was in the line shack playing cards."

"After Esteban Montoya was killed," the sheriff said.

"That could'a been anyone claimin' to be us," Elam said. He pointed to the wagons. "Besides, looks like Montoya's takin' the war to the folks in town as well."

"Elam, you got no proof Montoya was behind this," the sheriff replied.

"Who else would it be?" Elam asked.

"You heard Jesus same as the rest of us. These Mexicans are bandits with Bustamante."

"So what? You said it yourself, Sheriff. You never knew Bustamante to come across the border before."

The sheriff rubbed his chin and looked at the four dead bandits.

"No," he said slowly. "No, I reckon not."

"Well, there you have it. They come across the border because Montoya brought 'em across. Hell, it don't make no difference to him. All he cares about is stealin' as much land as he can grab off. If a few innocent folks get kilt along the way, well, so be it."

"Seems to me like it's gettin' a little out of hand on both sides," the sheriff said, looking at Quinn and the others. "Where'd you fellas come from?"

"Mississippi," Quinn said.

"Long ways. What're you doin' out here?"

"Maybe you didn't hear the news out here, Sheriff. South lost the war," Marcus said. "Didn't seem much to stay around for."

The sheriff rubbed his chin again as he looked at the five men who brought in the wagons.

"Yeah," he said. "All right, I reckon you got a point

there. Elam, all I got to say is, I don't want my town turned into a battlefield."

"The town ain't involved, Sheriff," Elam said easily. "No one's lookin' for trouble with the law."

"See to it," the sheriff said. He had made the statement for show and was relieved that Elam hadn't called him down on it. Now he was anxious to get out of here, so he started across the street to the undertaker to make arrangements for the burials. When the sheriff left, several others left as well, though there were many who stayed on, their morbid curiosity getting the better of them.

When Marcus and the others arrived at the Double X Ranch a couple of hours later, several of the cowhands turned out to see them. They had already seen Mason, and though he was a curiosity, he was unimpressive. Marcus and his men were different. Of course, the first man to arrest their attention was Billy Joe because of his tremendous size. Even the youngest and smallest of the group, Loomis, had an air of confidence that the hands noticed right away.

Marcus was a good judge of character. Some of the cowhands, he observed, were hard-working men who happened to be caught up in the range war. They had no particular ax to grind, no vested interest in the battle other than that they happened to be on one side or the other. In fact, they were not unlike many of the common soldiers Marcus and his men had encountered during the war. A private fought for Mississippi because he was born there. Had he been born in Ohio, he would have fought just as diligently for the Northern cause, which was true of the Yankee soldiers as well.

There were also people who had no interest other than the fact that they enjoyed the battle. Young, hot-blooded men who, because they were a thousand miles away from the war, didn't get the thirst for blood out of their systems. They were the ones he'd have to watch.

The first challenge came later that evening when Shorty—the champion rider, not only of the Double X, but of entire territory—asked Loomis if he had ever ridden in a horse race.

"A few," Loomis admitted. "I used to ride some in the county fairs back in Mississippi."

Loomis responded in such a low-key way that Shorty immediately jumped on it, hooting with derision over his "county fair" experience.

"Was they real horses, sonny? Or was they ponies?"

"No, they was mules," Deekus suggested. "You heard tell how he was from Mississippi. They don't have no horses in Mississippi, do they?"

Loomis didn't say anything.

Several people had gathered around the two men, listening in on their discussion. Bob, Billy, Joe, Hank, and Marcus were listening, too, but they weren't joining in the banter. They had heard it all before, so they just waited and watched what was going on.

"Tell me, sonny," Shorty went on. "Did you ever win any of those county-fair horse races you're talkin' about?"

"Sometimes."

"Even ridin' against full-growed men?"

"Shorty, ain't no men in Mississippi?" Deekus asked, and the others howled.

"You boys willin' set something up?" Marcus asked.

"Yeah, Shorty," one of the cowboys said, jumping on the suggestion. "Whyn't we set up a race an' show these here Southern whelps some real riding."

Within a moment others had taken up the suggestion and Loomis, by appearing to hesitate, made the cowboys howl even louder. Finally, as if he had been pushed into it against his will, Loomis agreed.

The race was no sooner set than the question of wagering came up. Every hand present had money to bet and Marcus and the others, pretending to be drawn into it as a matter of pride, covered all the bets.

"Come on down to the remuda, men," someone called. "We'll choose the mounts." All the cowboys rushed to the stable, leaving Marcus and his group behind. Marcus looked at the others, then they all laughed.

"How much have we got bet?" Bob asked.

"Better than two hundred dollars," Marcus said.

"Like taking candy from a baby," Hank commented.

Within an hour word of the impromptu race had traveled all over the ranch. Not only the cowboys, but the Chinese cook, Jim Harbin, Ike Elam, and his wife, Lucy, had come to watch the race. Marcus looked around to see if Julie was here, but he heard Harbin comment to someone that she was in town, working at the school.

The race course selected was obviously one that had been used before for that purpose. The horses would start by the barnyard gate, ride down to and around a stand of alamo trees about half a mile away, then return, the first one back through the gate the winner.

Because Shorty knew the string of horses, he picked the two they would ride. In order to keep it as fair as possible, they were to draw lots to determine who would ride which horse. When the two horses were brought up, Bob looked at them, then talked to them softly. Both horses whickered in his ear and he laughed.

"Them horses tell you somethin' funny, son?" Deekus asked.

Bob looked at Deekus and smiled. "They said it was too bad you weren't in this race."

"Why's that?" Deekus asked.

"'Cause then there'd be two horses and a jackass in the same race," Bob said. Everyone, including the cowboys, laughed. Deekus sulked off quietly.

"What do you think, Bob?" Loomis asked.

"Ain't a nickel's worth of difference between the two horses."

Lots were chosen by drawing straws. Shorty won the draw and chose the black horse, leaving the chestnut for Loomis. Loomis walked over and patted the chestnut on the neck, then saddled him. When he lifted the stirrups up very high, Shorty looked over at him curiously.

"What are you doin' that for?" he asked.

"Just my way of ridin'," Loomis answered. The cowboys looked at the strangely tied stirrups; some laughed but others wondered why he had done it, and how he would use them.

Shorty mounted his horse immediately and rode him over to the gate where they would start. Loomis led his animal over. Once there, Loomis had to have a boost up by his brother because the stirrups were so high. The sight of Loomis being hoisted onto the horse's back brought more laughter from the cowboys.

"Miz Elam," Curly called, "will you start this here race for us?" Several others took up the call, and Lucy Elam, who had been standing in the background, reluctantly walked out to the gate. She looked around at everyone, smiling broadly, until she happened to see Hank. For an instant their eyes held and she felt a flash of heat diffuse her body. She regained her composure quickly, however, and since the smile never left her face, no one realized it had happened. But Hank knew, and he let her know by his gaze.

"How will I do this?" Lucy asked.

"Here," Curly said, placing a pistol in her hand. "Just point this thing straight up in the air, say ready, set, then pull the trigger."

Lucy took the pistol awkwardly, then raised it in the air. "Ready," she said.

Now everyone knew why Loomis had adjusted the stirrups as he had. He put his feet in them, gripped the side of the horse with his knees, raised his butt up from the saddle, and leaned over the horse's neck. No one had ever seen any rider take such a position before, but many saw immediately that it would give the rider an advantage against the wind.

"Hey, wait a minute," Deekus said, but Lucy gave her next command, then pulled the trigger so quickly that Deekus was unable to finish whatever thought he had.

The two riders exploded forward, but almost immediately, Shorty veered his horse into Loomis, nearly knocking Loomis's horse down. At first Loomis thought it was an accident, but Shorty did it a second time, making it clear that it was intentional.

Loomis pulled his horse away from Shorty, which was what Shorty was looking for. He used the whip, and his own animal shot ahead like a bullet. Within an instant, Shorty was a full length ahead.

They were quite some distance from the crowd now, but Loomis could hear them shouting and cheering even over the pounding of hooves.

Shorty had several advantages. He knew the horse he was riding and he knew the course. He suddenly veered, aware of a patch of soft ground. Loomis rode right through it, and his horse buckled and nearly went down before he recovered. Now Shorty was two lengths ahead.

They reached the half-mile mark in just over a minute, rounded the trees, and started back. Now Loomis had the feel of his mount. He also knew the course since the last half mile was simply to go back over what he had just ridden across. Under his urging, his horse started to move up with long, rhythmic strides. His mount reached full speed and gradually closed the gap so that at the three-quarter mark they were head to head.

"Back off!" Shorty shouted. He reached across and lashed out at Loomis with his riding quirt. Loomis, seeing it coming, held his own quirt up and fended him off.

Bob was right about the horses—they were both competitive animals. When Shorty's horse saw Loomis's horse closing in on him, he increased his own pace, refusing to allow Loomis to pass. However, Loomis's horse was just as game and he hung in. As they approached the last eighth of a mile, both horses were still giving it all they had while the riders continued to fight with each other. Then Loomis began to ease ahead, inch by inch, then foot by foot. Shorty, realizing what was happening, stopped trying to use his whip on Loomis and began using it on his horse, lashing his flanks in furious desperation.

Shorty's horse responded well to the urging and began taking back some of the lead. But by now the last of Shorty's horse's reserves had been used up. Try as he might, he could not pick up the last nose ahead.

Both horses flashed across the finish line to the roar of those watching, but the winner, everyone agreed, was Loomis's horse, by a nose.

"You cheated me, you son of a bitch!" Shorty shouted, leaping down from his horse and starting angrily toward Loomis.

Loomis was off his horse instantly and turned to face Shorty.

"Hold on there, Shorty," Harbin said. "There wasn't no cheatin' here."

"Sure was. You seen how he fixed his stirrups like that. There ain't nothin' says you can do that."

"Far as I know, there ain't nothin' says you can't, neither," Harbin replied. "Sides, he did it before the race even started. You could've done it, if you had a mind too."

"Yeah, that's a fact," one of the other cowboys put in. "We're the ones lost the money on this here race and you don't hear none of us claimin' we was cheated. You was beat, Shorty, fair and square."

"Yeah, well, I don't like it," Shorty said, but he turned away and it was obvious that he had no intention of carrying his challenge or his protest any further. Whether it was because of Harbin or because of the quiet confidence he saw in Loomis's eyes, no one but Shorty knew.

Marcus watched the division of the cowboys. He could tell by the ones who went over to congratulate Loomis, or to look at the strange way he had tied off the stirrups, which of the men were going to be easy to get along with, and which of them were going to be trouble. It broke down about half and half. Harbin was the ranch foreman, and he was one of those who came over to congratulate Loomis. Deekus, who was the trail foreman, stayed with the others. Ike Elam, the owner, stayed aloof from it all.

Mason also didn't go with either group. He had watched the race, but he hadn't placed a wager on it. Now Marcus saw that the ugly little man was watching him, so he went over to speak to him.

"You got something to say, Mason?" Marcus asked.

"I was just rememberin' our meetin' a few days back."

"You wantin' to settle it right now?" Marcus asked.

"Naw, us being on the same side and all," Mason said with a humorless grin. "It'll keep." He turned and walked away.

Now some of the friendlier cowboys had found a bottle, and Marcus was invited to join the others in celebrating Loomis's victory. He watched Mason head toward the bunkhouse. He knew the time was going to come soon, when someone was going to have to kill the arrogant little bastard.

Nine

MARCUS WAS LYING on the bunk nearest the door. Earlier he had put his hat across his eyes to block out the light of the lantern from the table where half a dozen cowboys had played cards. The lantern was extinguished now, the cards put away, and most of the players snoring softly in their bunks. Loomis, Bob, and Billy Joe were asleep with the others, but when Hank started toward the door, Marcus pushed his hat back and called to him.

"Hank?"

"Yep."

"Are you going out there?"

"Yeah." There was a moment's pause, then Hank went on. "She'll be there, Marcus. You know she will."

"They always are," Marcus said. "Just that sometimes their husbands are, too."

"I reckon."

"But you're goin' anyway?"

"Yep."

Marcus sighed and pulled his hat back down. "Hope it's worth it," he said laconically.

It must be two o'clock in the morning, Lucy thought, and she was still unable to sleep. From Ike's room she could hear the steady sawing of his snores. After the drinking and partying that happened in the bunkhouse after the race, she was confident everyone on the ranch was asleep as well. She sighed, fluffed up the pillow, tried to find a more comfortable position, and closed her eyes. Sleep still would not come.

Finally she sat up. A bar of moonlight streamed in through the window, painting dappled shadows on the wall. Lucy got out of bed and walked over to the window, opened the curtains, and looked toward the bunkhouse.

He was in there, sleeping with the others. When she saw the new hand for the first time this afternoon, she knew. For the entire race, while everyone else was watching the horses and riders, she had eyes only for Hank Proudy.

Now it was the middle of the night, and there would never be a better time to have it happen than now. If only there was some way she could let him know that she was awake and willing.

Lucy looked beyond the bunkhouse, to the rolling hills of the pastureland, to the mesas and mountains beyond. The moon was so bright that she could see for miles, a landscape carved out in shades of silver and black.

On impulse, Lucy pulled a wrapper around her; then, barefooted but carrying her shoes with her, she stepped cautiously out of the room. The hall was thickly carpeted, and she could feel the carpet's rich texture beneath her feet as she walked silently down the length of the corridor. As she passed her husband's bedroom door she could hear him snoring loudly inside.

The house was dark, but a splash of moonlight coming in through the glass door at the foot of the stairs acted as a beacon to guide her. She moved slowly and silently down the stairs.

As she reached the landing she was startled by a sudden clicking noise followed by a whirring sound. Lucy froze as she felt her hair prickle, and she grabbed at the banister in sudden, numbing fear.

The clock chimed twice.

Lucy relaxed with a soft laugh.

At the front door Lucy slipped into her shoes, then went outside, down the porch steps, and onto the gravel paths. One of the paths led to the bunkhouse, one to the barn, and one led down to a gazebo, overlooking a well-tended flower garden. Lucy chose the path to the gazebo.

There was a gentle breeze blowing and it felt good as it moved through her hair and touched her skin. The breeze pressed the thin nightgown against her, and the nipples of her breasts stood out in bold relief.

"It's a beautiful night, isn't it?" a man's voice asked, its deep resonance startling her.

Hank had been leaning against the edge of the gazebo watching her approach. He knew she would be here, had known from the moment he first saw her this afternoon. He stepped out of the shadows and smiled.

"You surprised to see me out here, are you?"

"Mr. Proudy?"

"I figured if we were going to do it, this would be the best place," Hank said.

Lucy put her hand to her throat. "I . . . I don't know what on earth you are talking about, Mr. Proudy."

Hank chuckled a quiet, almost arrogant chuckle.

"Oh, I think you do," Hank said. He put his hands on her arms, feeling her skin through the thin cloth. "You came out here."

"I . . . I couldn't sleep. I thought I'd take some air," Lucy said.

"I'd be happy to help you," Hank whispered and reached down to unfasten her nightgown. When she didn't resist, he pulled it from her.

"Mr. Proudy!" she said and gasped. She was totally naked now.

Hank smiled and began unbuckling his belt.

"Don't you think we ought to be calling each other by our first names now, Lucy?" he asked. He let his trousers drop to the ground, then stood before her proudly, arrogantly erect.

When Lucy saw him she let out a gasp. There had been times during the last three years when she had cried herself to sleep in frustration with her husband. Now, before her, she saw what she had desired for so long, and all shame, all propriety fled, as she dropped to her knees before him.

"Oh," she said throatily as she wrapped her hands around his erection. "Is that for me?" She looked up at him, her eyes glowing brightly.

"Yes ma'am," Hank said. He reached down and touched the taut nipples of her breasts, feeling her shudder as he kneaded them gently.

"I hope you don't think I would do this for just anyone," Lucy said. She was so close to him now that, as she spoke, her warm breath moved across his skin like the most delicate silk.

In response, Hank put his hands down to her head and gently moved her to him. Her lips opened to take him. As she worked on him with her mouth his hands continued to tease her distended nipples.

He let her work on him for a few minutes, feeling the ripples of pleasure course through his body, stopping them at the last moment. Finally he pulled himself from her mouth. She looked up in surprise, hurt at being deprived.

"Let's do it," he said, pushing her gently down to the grassy knoll around the gazebo.

"Yes," she moaned.

Hank put his hand on her inner thigh, then moved it up. He slid his finger down through the lips of her sex. Hank's fingers teased, probed, stroked, and massaged until Lucy was squirming in uncontrollable desire.

"Please," Lucy said through clenched teeth. "Hank, now, can't you see? I can't wait anymore."

Hank moved over her, then went in, feeling the

delicious sensation of total invasion. As she writhed in ecstasy beneath him, he put his mouth to her neck. He could feel her neck muscles twitching, and he opened his mouth to suck on the creamy white flesh. He could hear the gasps and moans of pleasure from this beautiful creature beneath him, and she continued to raise her hips wildly to meet his every thrust.

Lucy's gasps and moans rose in intensity, and Hank knew by the increased thrashing of her hips, the spasmodic action of her body, that she was nearing orgasm. He stayed with her, and when her orgasm hit, the contractions of her sex pulled at him, sucking the juices from deep within Hank's body. When they were both spent and satiated, they lay naked and breathless under the full moon.

At that same moment, but several miles away, on Rancho Montoya, a small figure walked fearfully into a darkened bedroom. "Señor Montoya," he whispered loudly. "Señor Montoya, please wake up."

When Juan opened his eyes, he saw his houseboy, Carlos, standing by his bed, a serape wrapped around the underwear he used as pajamas. Carlos's eyes were wide and shining with excitement or fear, maybe a little of both. Juan had no idea what time it was, but from the position of the moon he knew it had to be two or three in the morning, certainly an unusual time to be called.

"What is it, Carlos?" Juan asked. "Why have you awakened me at this hour?"

"Please forgive me for disturbing your sleep, Excelente, but there is an hombre at the front door with a message for you," Carlos said.

Juan ran his hand through his hair sleepily. "A message for me? Why do you bother me at this hour?"

"Excelente, he would not deliver the message to me. He said it must be for you only."

Juan pointed to his robe, an elegant garment of purple silk. The coat of arms of the Montoya family, a plumed helmet above a lion rampant, was embroidered in gold on the left pocket.

"I must tell you one thing more," Carlos said as he helped Juan into the robe.

"*Si?*"

"The man with the message is a bandito. I am sure he is from one of the bands in Mexico."

Juan looked around sharply. "Are there more?" he asked.

"I do not think there are more, Excelente. Before I came in to see you I looked through the upstairs window. There is only one horse. I am sure he is alone."

Juan opened the top drawer of the chifforobe and pulled out a small pocket derringer. Charging the two barrels with powder and ball, he slipped the little gun into his pocket. The derringer, he knew, was not accurate beyond a few feet, but within that space its .41-caliber bullet was extremely deadly. He nodded at Carlos.

"All right, let's see what our bandito friend wants," he said. He patted his pocket. "And if he is too disagreeable, I have the means to deal with him."

Lamps burned in the hallway and on the stairs, so Juan's way was illuminated. When he reached the landing he stood at the top of the stairs and looked down on the great room and his visitor.

The night intruder seemed visibly impressed with the room, and he stood just inside the door holding his sombrero in his hands, looking at the richly paneled walls, cathedral ceiling, hanging tapestries, heavy furniture, candelabras, and polished lanterns. Juan was glad to see the awe with which the messenger was taking it all in, because it meant that his visitor was a peasant whose normal reaction was to be cowed by wealth and position. He decided to use that to his advantage.

"What do you mean by calling at this hour of the morning?" Juan asked in his most commanding voice.

The visitor looked around, saw the elegant robe and the commanding presence of the master of the house, and he blanched visibly.

"I beg your forgiveness, Excelente," the visitor said, bowing slightly. "I was sent here by my chief, General Pedro Bustamante."

Carlos was correct, Juan thought. He said the messenger looked as if he rode with a bandito band. Every two-peso bandit in Mexico who could get half a dozen men to follow him called himself a general.

At first Juan started to make a derisive comment about it; then he decided not to. It was obvious his visitor was impressed by title and position; it wouldn't do to undermine that sense of inferiority, even if it meant acting as if the general deserved the messenger's respect.

"And what is so important that the general wishes to tell me about it at this hour?" Juan asked.

"The general wishes to meet with you, Excelente. He asks that you come to the Sombrero Boulder at Le Tigre Pass. He asks that you do this alone."

"What is the meeting about?"

"I do not know, Excelente," the bandito said.

Juan ran his hand through his hair. The place Bustamante chose to meet him was very isolated, its approaches easily seen. There was no way Juan could have someone go with him without being seen. If Bustamante wanted to do anything to him, Juan would be helpless to resist.

On the other hand, if he didn't go, Bustamante could attack the ranch, perhaps harm his family. He had enough trouble with the Double X and didn't need to be facing the possibility of an attack by bandits as well. The best thing would be to see what the man wanted.

"When is this meeting to take place?"

"At midmorning, Excelente."

"Very well. You may return to the general and tell him I will be there."

The sun was one-quarter of the way through its daily sojourn when Juan Montoya reached Sombrero Boulder. There he saw three men waiting in the shade of the overhanging slab that gave the boulder its name. They came out to meet him.

"Don Juan de la Montoya, I am General Pedro Bustamante, at your service," Pedro said. He took off his sombrero and made a sweeping bow.

Juan looked at Pedro and at the two men with him. He had never seen anyone as heavily armed as these three men were. Between them they had six pistols, three rifles, and three knives. They were also a walking armory of ammunition.

"What can I do for you, General?" Juan asked.

Bustamante smiled broadly when Juan called him General.

"No, no, Excelente," Pedro said, wagging his finger back and forth. "It is not what you can do for me, but what I, General Pedro Bustamante, can do for you. I can help you win your war."

"What war?"

Pedro forced a laugh. He looked at the two men who were with him, and they laughed as well—high, insane cackles. "What war? Ah, you say what war when everyone knows of the war being fought between Rancho Montoya and the Double X Ranch."

"Why would you want to fight in this war?"

"Because, Excelente, I am fired with patriotic zeal when I think of the slaughter of your poor brother. Your brother was a hero who defeated a terrible bandito and did me a great personal favor since this bandito made claims on a territory that is under my control."

"Perhaps so, but this is a private war."

"No, señor, it is not a private war. It is a war between my fellow countrymen and the gringos."

"General, very few of your people are involved. We are all Americans, the vaqueros of Rancho Montoya and the cowboys of Double X Ranch. So as I say, it is a private war that concerns only us."

"But you are wrong. It is my war, too, patriotism or no."

"How is this so?"

"It is my war because of the murder of my men," Pedro said. "Four men, innocent travelers who happened upon the dead drivers of two freight wagons, were set upon by five gringos who burst upon them like demons from hell, shooting them down without so much as one question. Now I ask you, Excelente, what of my men?"

"I have heard of these innocent travelers," Juan said. "I have heard they killed the wagon men and were stealing the goods when they were set upon by the five gringos."

"But this is not true. Do you think my men would steal such things as were in those wagons? Bah!" Pedro said, spitting on the ground. "It would shame them . . . it would shame me, their general, for them to steal washboards and women's corsets."

"Perhaps so," Juan agreed, deciding it was better to keep his real opinion to himself. "But whatever happened to your men is of no consequence to the war between Señor Elam and myself. I thank you for your kind offer of help, but I will not need it."

"You do not take my offer, even though you know that the five gringos who killed my poor men have gone to work for Elam?"

"Again, General, I thank you for your offer," Juan said. "But I must decline."

Pedro's eyes narrowed, and for one long moment Juan thought it was going to become a shootout. Then, suddenly and inexplicably, Pedro laughed. As before when he laughed, his two companions laughed with him.

"Very well, Don Juan de la Montoya. Fight the war

by yourself, but when you find that things are not as you wish them to be, do not come to me for help. By then it will be too late."

"I understand," Juan said. He turned and walked to his horse with every muscle in his body twitching. He could almost feel a gun pointed at his back and he wondered if he would live to mount his horse or if Pedro would shoot him down.

"Excelente," Pedro called.

Here it comes, Juan thought, and he bunched the muscles between his shoulders, as if by that action he could stop a bullet.

"Yes?" he answered without turning around.

"Via con Dios, señor."

"Si, General. *Via con Dios."*

Ten

JULIE DIPPED A cloth in the bucket of water, then began washing the blackboards in the single-room schoolhouse where she taught. When Marcus Quinn and his friends brought in the two wagons last week, she had stayed back in the emporium. Even when Lucy went running out into the street to join the others, she had stayed back because she didn't want to see Marcus. She didn't think she could face the shame of seeing him again.

As she recalled that night her blood warmed and her breathing grew shallow. Oh, how wonderful it had been . . . how much she wished she could do it again. If only he were here, right now, they could pull the shades, lock the doors. No one would see them, no one would know.

And then, when she realized the extent of her thoughts, her face flamed in embarrassment and she dipped the cloth in the bucket and began washing the blackboard with renewed vigor.

"Miss Harbin?"

Julie covered the board with broad sweeps, watching the slate grow black under each pass as the white film of chalk was cleaned away.

"Miss Harbin?"

Julie suddenly realized that someone was calling her name, had actually called her twice, though she had been so lost in her own thoughts that it just now got through to her. She turned toward the sound and saw a beautiful young Mexican girl standing just inside the doorway of the schoolhouse.

"Yes?" Julie asked. She put the cloth back in the bucket.

"Excuse me, Miss Harbin, for interrupting you," the girl said. "You are a teacher and are busy."

Julie laughed and pointed to the blackboard, half cleaned, half dusted with chalk. "I'd hardly call this very important. Believe me, it's work that can be interrupted," she said.

"I call your name but you do not hear me."

"I'm sorry I didn't hear you the first time. I was lost in thought." She ran her hand through her hair and cleared her throat, then made a motion of invitation with her hand. "Please, come in. What can I do for you?"

The girl came into the room and at Julie's invitation, sat at one of the desks. She looked around the room and smiled. "It is nice, your school," she said.

"Thank you."

"My name is Doña Carlotta Maria de Alarcon Sanchez."

"Heavens, that's quite a name," Julie teased.

Carlotta laughed, her black eyes flashing, then she blushed. "I am told it is proper to tell a teacher the full name. I am called Carlotta."

Suddenly Julie realized who Carlotta was, and the smile left her face, replaced by a look of concern.

"Oh, you poor child," she said. "You were the fiancée of Señor Montoya's brother, weren't you?"

"*Si*," Carlotta said, her eyes darting down quickly, covered by lashes that were as long and as delicate as a black lace fan.

"I was so sorry to hear about that," Julie said. "I don't know who did it, but I do hope they are caught and punished."

"Please, Miss Harbin, these are bad times," Carlotta said. "Our men are in—how do you say?—*los campos opuestos?*"

"Opposite camps," Julie said.

"*Si*," Carlotta said, nodding. She smiled. "But I think we are not enemies."

Julie smiled broadly. "I agree," she said. "Let the men be foolish if they wish. We need not be. Now, tell me, Carlotta. What can I do for you?"

Carlotta folded her hands on the desk in front of her.

"I ask to go to your school," she said.

"You?"

"*Si*. I can read and write my language and some in English. I wish to learn more."

"Oh, I don't know," Julie said. "My students are much younger—from the first grade to the eighth. I don't have the books for someone your age."

"Please, Miss Harbin," Carlotta interrupted. "I am

older, yes, but I do not have much school. My father took me from the school and made me learn many other things . . . how to act like a lady, how to make lace, how to smile and dance for the men."

Julie smiled.

"But now I wish to learn things I can use," Carlotta continued. "If you say yes, I will work hard for you. I will help you watch over the little ones, I will scrub the blackboard for you, I will carry books, I—"

Julie laughed and held up her hand. "Oh, now, it isn't necessary for you to do all that," she said. "If you wish to attend my school, I will be very happy to have you."

Carlotta let out a squeal of delight. "Oh, thank you!"

"Be here tomorrow morning," she said.

"I will be," Carlotta promised. She got up from the desk and hurried to the door, then stopped and looked back. The happy smile on her face was temporarily gone, replaced with a more serious look. "And, Miss Harbin?"

Julie looked up at her. "Yes?"

"Let us say that here, in this classroom, all of us, Mexican or gringo, will be with friends."

Julie agreed, smiling warmly.

Carlotta's face lit up in another smile, then she waved happily and left the building.

Mason stood just inside the livery stable across the street from the school. The bottom half of the door was closed and he leaned on it, looking through the open top half. From here, he had discovered, he could see into the school, and when Julie Harbin was at her desk, or at the blackboard, he could see her.

In the two weeks since Mason had arrived in Diablo, the Harbin girl had spoken to him only in the most perfunctory way. Sometimes he would watch carefully, judging exactly when she would leave the school, then he would hurry to get into position to walk by her. He always made it a point to tip his hat and speak, and she answered him with a polite nod of her head, but never once had they exchanged any pleasantries.

Who does she think she is? he wondered. Men quaked in their boots when they saw him. He once made a six-foot-tall, powerfully built man get on his knees and beg for his life, relishing the thought of reducing such a fine specimen of manhood to a quivering lump of jelly.

Then he blew his brains out.

"You are in that schoolhouse all alone some evenings, ain't you, missy?" he said under his breath. "Well, little miss high-and-mighty bitch, let's see what you're like some late night when you think you're safe, when there's nobody around for you to turn to. You'll notice me then. Yes, ma'am, I can guarantee that you will notice me than. I'll make you beg me to use you any way I want to. I'll make you beg me not to kill you. Then maybe, just maybe, if you're really good to me, I'll let you live."

It took less than a week for Quinn and the others to realize that the situation here presented them with an opportunity to make some money beyond their fee from Ike Elam. It was obvious that Elam was stealing cattle from Montoya, and Montoya was stealing cattle from Elam. That was one of the first things they discovered. With so many stolen cattle moving back and forth, it seemed an easy enough task to get hold of some. Also, Bob found a secluded box canyon far enough away from the normal range of the Double X cowboys and Montoya vaqueros, to allow the boys to hide a few head on their own.

"The way I see it," Marcus explained to the others, "Elam hired us to protect his cattle and look after his water and line shacks, right?"

"Right," the others agreed.

Marcus smiled. "As near as I can remember, he didn't say nothin' at all about us protecting the cattle he steals from Montoya."

"I sure didn't hear him say nothin' like that," Bob said, smiling broadly.

"So what exactly you got in mind?" Hank asked.

"I figure any of Montoya's cows that Elam has stolen are fair game for us," Marcus explained.

"Sounds good enough," Loomis agreed. "But what do we do with them when we got them?"

Marcus looked at Hank and held out his hand toward him.

"Boys, I want you to meet Mr. Manley Luscom, cattle dealer from the U.S. Government. Hank, you think you can find an outfit in those fancy duds you have that'll make someone in the Mexican government believe you're an official cattle dealer?"

"Reckon I can," Hank agreed.

"Good. Get all prettied up and ride down to Fronteras. Get the best price you can."

"Won't the Mexican government start askin' questions when two different brands show up in the same shipment?" Billy Joe asked.

"Don't worry about me, boys," Hank bragged. "Them Mexicans'll be eatin' outta my hand."

Late the next afternoon Hank Proudy, passing himself off as Manley Luscom, cattle dealer for the U.S. government, swung down from his horse and snapped his fingers at a Mexican private.

"You, Private," he said irritably. "Is this any way to greet a man who has the endorsement of His Excellency, Emperor Maximilian? Take care of my horse at once."

At the sound of Maximilian's name, the soldier moved quickly to take the reins from the fancily dressed man who spoke with such authority. A captain, seeing this, moved quickly to address Hank.

"I beg your pardon, señor," he said. "But who are you and what are you doing here?"

"What am I doing here?" Hank asked. He looked around the sleeping little Mexican village, then at the barracks where the troops were billeted. A Mexican flag hung limply from one pole, a French flag from another. "I am here at the invitation of your government. Now I have a question for *you*, señor." Hank fixed his most imperial gaze upon the captain. "Why wasn't I met by a military escort as the emperor promised?" he thundered.

"I'm sorry, señor," the Mexican captain answered, obviously cowed by Hank's demeanor. He spoke in rapid Spanish and soldiers started running in all directions.

"Where is your commanding officer?" Hank asked.

"Please, señor, this way," the captain said. "I have sent for the colonel."

Hank followed the captain into the barracks. The captain showed him into an elegant reception room where he was met by a white-jacketed orderly and shown to a table. Another orderly poured a glass of brandy for him.

"Well, now," Hank said, holding up the glass and letting it catch a sunbeam to explode in a brilliant burst of light. "This is more like it."

The captain and orderlies left Hank alone for a few moments and he leaned back in the chair to look around the room. A picture of Maximilian hung on one wall, Napoleon the Third on another. He saw a humidor of fine cigars on the table and he took four, putting three of them in his pocket, then biting the tip off the fourth. He looked for a cuspidor and seeing none, spit the end on the carpet. He had just lit it when the commanding officer breezed in, still buttoning his tunic, exchanging rapid Spanish with the captain who had shown Hank in.

"I am Colonel Antonio Morales, señor," the colonel said, drawing to a stop in front of Hank and clicking his heels together ceremoniously. The captain stood at rigid attention behind his colonel, the orderlies behind the captain.

"Ah, yes, Colonel Morales," Hank said. He examined the end of his cigar for a moment then held it up. "An excellent cigar, señor. But then, Maximilian did say that you were a man of good taste."

Colonel Morales smiled broadly. "The emperor mentioned my name?"

"That he did, Colonel, that he did," Hank said. "When he told me to set up this cattle deal, he specified Colonel Antonio Morales. So here I am."

Colonel Morales saw that Hank's brandy glass was nearly empty and he snapped his fingers at one of the orderlies. The orderly picked up the brandy decanter and Hank's snifter was refilled.

"Señor, I am most embarrassed," Colonel Morales said. "But His Excellency has not contacted me about you. I must confess that I do not know what this is about."

"Surely, Colonel, you jest," Hank said, looking at the Mexican in surprise. "You have not been told of my mission?"

"No, señor."

Hank got up and set his glass on the table. "I'm sorry," he said. "Perhaps I should return at another time."

"No, no, señor," the colonel said quickly. "If you would tell me what the emperor expects of me, I am certain we can follow your orders."

"I don't know," Hank said. "When I deal with someone, I have to know that he has the authority to make the deal stick."

Colonel Morales drew himself up to his full five feet six-inch height. "Señor, you may rest assured that I, Colonel Antonio Morales, have the authority you seek."

Hank smiled and reached for his glass. "All right, Colonel. It's cattle."

"Cattle, señor?"

"Yes. I am here to offer you prime beef on the hoof for ten dollars a head."

"But I don't understand. What am I to do with this beef?"

"Why, you're going to resell it to the Mexican government for fifteen dollars a head," Hank said. "The government is going to love you for getting such a bargain on cattle—that's five dollars under the going market—and you're going to make five dollars a head besides. Colonel Morales, you're going to be a rich man."

Morales did a quick calculation in his head, then he smiled broadly. "Señor, you are certain you can make these cattle available?"

"Absolutely," Hank said. "Are you certain you can come up with ten dollars a head?"

Morales turned to his captain and the two orderlies and, in Spanish, ordered them from the room. He closed the door behind them, then dropped the bar in place. He turned to look at Hank.

"Señor, in two weeks I will have the payroll for every military person in northern Sonora. I will use money from that payroll to pay for the cattle. Once I have sold the cattle to my government, I will replace the money."

Hank smiled and held up his finger. "Ah, but not all of it, right, Colonel? Remember, five dollars per head is your profit."

"*Si*," Colonel Morales said. "Five dollars per head is my profit." He poured himself a glass of brandy, then held it up to click it against Hank's glass. "To cattle, señor. And a profitable business between our two great countries."

Hank laughed. "Our countries hell," he said. "I'm

drinking to a profitable business between Colonel Antonio Morales and Manley Luscom."

"And what our countries do not know, will not hurt them, eh, Señor Luscom."

"Believe me, Colonel, they'll never feel a thing," Hank said, raising the glass to his lips.

When Hank returned to the Double X Ranch, he was met by Marcus and the others.

"We got a deal," he said. "All we need now are a few cows."

"Bob's got it all figured," Marcus said.

"We've got fifteen head in the box canyon already," Bob said. "And me an' my brother seen another five head of Montoya cows down by the south breaks."

"That's two hundred dollars right there," Hank said. "Damn, boys, this could turn into something real profitable."

Eleven

BOB WANTED TO check out the New York Saloon to see what they had in the way of soiled doves. Billy Joe had already eaten the supper the cook had fixed, but he felt like having something more, so the idea of spending a little time in town seemed pleasant enough to him. The two men rode into Diablo together.

The sun was setting as they moved down Main Street. The buildings cast long shadows across the road. The first building they passed was the stable. They had been in town on the day they brought the wagons in, but this was the first time they had been back since they arrived.

Across the street from the stable was the school, then a boot and leather store, gun shop, barbershop, emporium, a few cantinas, a couple of restaurants, a place called "Vi's Pies," the sheriff's telegraph office, and the New York Saloon. Scattered behind the main row of commercial buildings were a handful of little houses.

"You sure you don't want to get something to eat later, Billy Joe?" Bob asked. "We could get us a couple of girls at the Saloon, go upstairs for a while, then come on down to one of them restaurants later."

"How's about you find yourself a girl and I go find me some real food?"

Bob chuckled. "I don't understand a man who'd rather eat than screw."

"I reckon I just don't like to ride in the saddle that's been soaped up for me."

Bob laughed out loud. "Ah, Billy Joe, you just don't 'ppreciate the finer points."

"Vi's Pies," Billy Joe said.

"Huh?"

"Vi's Pies." Billy Joe pointed to the sign, then angled his horse over toward the hitching rail in front. "I think I'll try a few of them an' see how they are."

"All right," Bob said, shaking his head. "See you later."

Billy Joe stepped down from his horse in front of Vi's Pies while Bob walked on down a few feet to the New York Saloon. Billy Joe tied his horse, then went inside.

A little bell on the door rang as he pushed it open.

"Be right with you," a woman's voice called.

Billy Joe sat at a table and breathed deeply of the delicious aroma. He smelled apples, cinnamon, cherries, flour, and nutmeg.

"Now what will it be?" a woman asked, stepping into the dining room from the kitchen. The woman was tall and blond, not fat but big boned. She was wearing an apron and she smelled of sugar and cinnamon. She smiled at Billy Joe and fussed her hair.

"How do, ma'am?"

"Well, how do yourself, stranger. My name's Violet Simmons. Most folks call me Vi."

Billy Joe smiled engagingly. He had never seen a more beautiful woman, had never smelled a woman with such delicious scents.

"I want pie, ma'am."

Vi laughed. "I have all kinds of pie. What kind do you want?"

"Slice of each."

Vi gasped. "I don't take to jokes about my business, mister."

"I ain't jokin'," Billy Joe said, taking a coin out of his pants and putting it on the table.

"Honey, if you can eat one slice of each kind of pie I've got in here, you can have it all free."

"Suits me fine," Billy Joe agreed happily.

"Coming right up."

As Billy Joe was sitting down to his pie, Jim Harbin, after a ride of a couple of hours, was just approaching Naco. The sun was down now, and the night creatures were calling to each other. A cloud passed over the moon, then moved away, bathing in silver the little town that rose up before him. Two dozen adobe buildings, half of which spilled yellow light onto the ground out front, faced the town plaza. The building that was the biggest and most brightly lit was the single cantina in the town.

As he drew nearer to town, Harbin could hear someone playing a guitar inside the cantina. It was a mournful sound which caused him to shiver involuntarily. When he was a kid they used to say that such a shiver meant someone had just stepped on a grave. He put it out of his mind.

Harbin stopped his horse just at the edge of town, then ground-hobbled him. He decided to walk into town, believing that a man afoot would make a quieter entrance than a man on horseback. He didn't want to draw attention.

The smell of beans and spicy beef from one of the houses hung in the night air. A dog barked somewhere, but its bark was quickly silenced by an impatient owner, more interested in quiet than in investigating what caused the dog to bark.

A baby cried.

As Harbin moved through the little town, through the patches of light and shadow, he thought of the conversation he had overheard this afternoon. Ike Elam had called Deekus over to talk to him. Harbin was working on a halter just on the other side of the barn door so as the two men spoke, they were unaware that he was nearby, listening to them.

"I'll be meetin' with Pedro Bustamante at the cantina in Naco," Elam had said.

"That's that Mexican bandit fella, ain't it? The one that calls hisself a general?"

"Yeah."

"What do you think, boss? What's this here Mexican fella want?"

"The message I got said that he has a deal. I figure it has something to do with Montoya."

"You think you can trust him?"

Elam chuckled. "That's not the question," he replied. "I'd make a deal with the devil himself right now if it meant runnin' Montoya out of here."

Harbin wasn't supposed to know about the meeting. But now he did know and, with any luck, tonight he would be able to find out just what was going on. He didn't mind fighting for Elam, if Elam was honest. But if Elam wasn't playing fair, he wanted no part of it.

Harbin reached the cantina. There, in the lantern light that spilled through the door, he saw Elam's horse. Harbin moved up to the horse and patted it on the neck. The horse, recognizing Harbin's smell, nodded his head at the greeting.

Harbin listened to the sounds from the cantina. The music had stopped and now there was only conversation, Mexican mostly, but then he heard Ike Elam's voice. Harbin looked up and down the street to make certain no one was watching the cantina door, then he stepped up onto the board porch and pushed his way inside.

Pulling his hat brim low, he headed straight for the bar and positioned himself in the middle of a group of men so he wouldn't be seen. He glanced across the room and spied Elam in a far corner, sitting at a table. Across the table from him was a Mexican, and from the descriptions he had heard, the Mexican was General Pedro Bustamante. The two men were talking, and as their words were virtually the only English being spoken in the entire Cantina, the words seemed to rise above the din of Spanish so Harbin could hear them quite easily.

"We will make a good team, you and I, señor," Bustamante was saying. "You will fight the Montoyas above the border—I will fight them below."

"Yeah, well the thing is, General, I don't give a shit what happens to Montoya below the border. He can own every inch of land between here and Mexico City as far as I'm concerned."

"I see. So you want my men to attack on this side of the border as well, is this so?"

"Yes."

"Then for this you must pay well."

"I thought Montoya was your enemy. Why should I pay you for fightin' him?"

"Señor, you must understand, I am a revolutionaire. I am fighting against Maximilian, the ruler the French have put upon the necks of my people. For this battle I need money to buy weapons and food for my soldiers. But, señor, if I am to fight on this side of the border, it is very dangerous for me. How will it look to your country for me, a general in the Revolutionary Army of Mexico, to attack a rich American?"

"All right," Elam said. "All right, suppose I say to you that I will pay you two dollars for every head of Montoya cattle you deliver to me?"

"I can get more money from the same cattle by taking them across the border and selling them in my country."

"Yes, but you have to get them across the border. This way you only have to get them to me. I'll take care of the rest."

"Very well, señor, we have a deal," Bustamante said, smiling broadly.

One of Bustamante's soldiers walked across the room and leaned over to whisper something to his leader. Bustamante nodded, then spoke to Elam again.

"Señor, I have been told that a gringo is at the bar, listening to our conversation. Is he a friend of yours?"

When Harbin heard that, he turned quickly and was about to leave, but his way was barred by two of Bustamante's men.

"Harbin?" Elam called, standing up from the table and crossing over to the bar. He had an angry expression on his face. "Harbin, what the hell are you doing here?"

"I just stopped in for a drink," Harbin said. "Then when I saw you were busy I thought I should wait over here until you were through." Harbin smiled. "I reckon you're finished now, so what say we have a drink?"

"What did you hear?" Elam asked.

"Why, nothin'," Harbin said. "I didn't hear nothin' you an' that fella was talkin' about."

Elam looked over into the corner and nodded, a barely perceptible move of his head.

"Oh, I think you heard every word, Jim. I think now you're planning on going back and spreading it around to the others that I've made a deal with General Bustamante."

Harbin sighed. It was out now—he could no longer pretend he didn't know.

"All right," he admitted. "I heard your damn plan.

I'm goin' to tell the other ranchers in the valley, and I'm goin' to write a letter to the territorial governor. What you're plannin' ain't right, Elam. I worked for you, and I helped you hire guns, even when it went against my grain. But I'm not goin' to stand by and watch you bring in somebody like Pedro Bustamante to do your killin' for you."

"I see," Elam said. "I don't suppose it would do any good to tell you to get on your horse and ride away."

"Ride away where?"

"Out of the territory. Go to Texas or up to Colorado. You can send for your daughter later, and I'll pay for it."

"I ain't goin' anywhere, Elam."

"I was afraid of that," Elam said. He sighed, then nodded toward the corner.

Mason was in the corner of the cantina, playing a game of solitaire. When he saw Elam nod at him, he stood up and moved to the center of the room.

"Mr. Mason, I think you'd better take care of this," Elam said.

"What are you talking about?" Harbin asked nervously.

Harbin knew what Elam was talking about, and so did everyone else in the cantina—even those people who spoke no English. They knew by the expression in the voice, by the look on the face, by the catlike moves of the ugly little man with the big gun.

"Mr. Harbin, I see you're not wearin' a gun. Maybe you better get one," Mason suggested.

"I'm a workin' hand, Mason, not a gunfighter," Harbin said.

"Someone give him a gun," Mason said coldly.

Elam took his gun out and put it on the bar next to Harbin. "I'm sorry, Jim," he said. "You brought it to this . . . you left me no choice."

"Don't be apologizing to me, Elam," Harbin said. "I don't intend to pick the gun up."

"I think you will," Mason said.

"Mason, you're on American soil. This cantina is full of witnesses. Not even you would kill a man in cold blood in front of dozens of witnesses."

Without another word Mason pulled his gun and fired, then replaced it in his holster. He did it so quickly that nobody had any idea what was about to happen, least of all Harbin, who felt the sudden sting of the bullet as it took away his left earlobe. He jerked his hand up, felt the raw meat at the bottom of the ear, then pulled it away full of sticky blood.

"You son of a bitch!" Harbin cursed.

"Use the gun, Harbin," Mason said.

"No."

Again the gun was out, another flash of flame, a roar, and Harbin was now missing two earlobes. He didn't put his hand up to this one, but just stood there as blood ran down both cheeks.

"Use it," Mason said again.

"You got your gun in a holster," Harbin finally said. "That gives you an advantage."

"Pick it up or I'll shoot you down right now," Mason said.

Harbin shook his head no.

"What does it take to make you a man?" Mason asked. Then he smiled. "Maybe if I tell you about your daughter, how I—"

"Leave Julie out of this."

Mason's smile broadened. He had found how he could get to Harbin, force him into a shooting match.

"Maybe you want to stay around a little longer so you can watch me have your daughter. She wants me, Harbin. I've seen the way she looks at me, I've seen that hungry look in women's eyes before. She wants what I've got for her." He reached around with his left hand and grabbed himself.

"Shut up, you foul-mouthed bastard."

"Well, now, Mr. Harbin. You can shut me up. You can shut me up and protect that little girl of yours at the same time. If you get lucky, just real lucky, you might . . ."

Suddenly, desperately, Harbin made a clawing grab for the pistol. Mason drew his gun and had it pointed at Harbin before the man could even lift the pistol from the bar. Mason stopped and smiled. For just a moment the two men formed a bizarre tableau, then Mason pulled the trigger.

The bullet caught Harbin in the throat and he dropped the gun unfired, then clutched at his neck. Blood spilled between his fingers and he let out a gurgling death rattle. He fell against the bar, then slid down, dead before he reached the floor.

The patrons of the bar who had moved out of the way at the start of the confrontation, and who had ducked in fear at the two bullets that cut off Harbin's earlobes, now began moving carefully back to the bar. All of them looked at the prostrate form of Jim Harbin, his sightless eyes open, his mouth in a grimace of anger, the gaping wound in his throat oozing red with blood. His arms were lying to either side, fingernails broken and dirty, palms callused. He had been a working man all his life and everything about his body showed that. His pants and shirt, while clean, were well worn, skillfully patched here and there by his own hand.

A dozen or more of the Mexican patrons crossed themselves and a few even mumbled a prayer for him.

Twelve

WHEN BOB WENT into the New York Saloon he discovered that two of the girls had already gone upstairs for the night. There was a third girl left to work the trade, but Bob took one look at her and decided he wouldn't take her to a dogfight. He went over to the bar and stood there nursing a beer and brooding over his bad luck.

"She ain't much," the man next to him said.

"What?"

"Linda. I seen you lookin' at her. She ain't exactly the kind of woman a man wants to belly up to, 'lessen it's been a long, dry spell." He chuckled.

"You're right about that," Bob said.

"Try Rosita," the man suggested.

"Rosita?" Bob looked around. "I don't see no other girls."

"No, she ain't in here. She works at the Seguines

Cantina across the street. Believe me, she'll ride you hard and put you away wet. I know 'cause I done tried 'er."

Bob thought about it for a moment, then drained the rest of his beer and set the mug down.

"All right, mister, I'm gonna give Rosita a try," he said. "Much obliged."

Across the street in Seguines, Rosita looked particularly alluring this evening. She had black flashing eyes, ruby lips, and teeth as white as pearls. Her long blue-black hair was tied back with a red ribbon, which matched the color of the sash at her waist. The dress she was wearing was very low cut and particularly revealing, so when she served Bob his drink and leaned over his table, she treated him to a more than generous view of her breasts.

With all the skills of her profession, Rosita engaged in the art of seduction, running her fingers along his jawline, brushing her hips against his arm. Within a few more visits to his table, aided by a little squeeze here and a tiny pressure there, she accomplished what she set out to do. Bob made the suggestion, she quoted a price, and the two of them went up the stairs together. About halfway up the stairs he glanced over at the bar and caught a glimpse of the man he had met in the New York Saloon. He held up his glass of tequila in silent salute, and Bob smiled down at him.

When they reached the top of the stairs, Rosita called out in Spanish, and a short, heavyset woman hurried down the hall. She opened a door, then stepped away from it.

"Señor," Rosita said, holding her arm toward the open door, smiling in broad invitation.

"Where I come from it's ladies first," Bob said.

"You are a fine gentleman," Rosita said, stepping into the room just ahead of him. Bob followed her, and once inside saw a bed, bedside table, chair, and chifforobe. The heavyset woman Rosita had spoken to hurried over to the chifforobe where there was a pitcher, bowl, and towel. She filled the bowl with water from the pitcher, then turned and started to back out of the room. Just before she left, Rosita said something else to her. The woman's eyes grew wide for an instant, then Rosita spoke again, more sharply this time, and the woman nodded.

"*Si*," she said very quietly.

"Is something wrong?" Bob asked, surprised by the sharpness of the words he couldn't understand.

"Maria is a stupid woman," Rosita said. "Every time I must give her instructions—every time she does not obey."

"Maybe I'd better—" Bob started to say, but Rosita reached up to touch him.

"No," she said, shaking her head and pouting. "It is nothing. You will not leave Rosita alone, will you?"

"No," Bob said, wondering how the coolness of her fingers on his neck could so heat his blood. "I'm not going anywhere."

Rosita smiled in triumph, then undid the ribbon that held her hair. She shook her head to let it come down.

She gave him a long seductive look, then frowned. "How can we make love if you wear all your clothes?"

She helped Bob remove his clothes. Then, lying back on the bed naked, he watched as Rosita began undressing before him.

Rosita, who had already demonstrated her skill in the art of seduction downstairs, knew instinctively that it could best be continued by appealing to his eyes. Half closing her long-lashed lids over her dark eyes, she began removing her clothes, pulling the dress off her shoulders and pushing it down her body, treating him with slow, teasing moves. She was an exceptionally beautiful woman, and he enjoyed seeing her firm, well-rounded breasts. The dark nipples were drawn tight by their exposure to the air.

Continuing the seductive dance, Rosita pushed the dress farther down on her body, exposing more of the smooth, bare skin until he could see the pinch of her navel, then the triangle of dark hair that curled invitingly at the junction of her thighs. Finally the dress fell to the floor, a rustling pool of taffeta, and she stepped out of it and glided over to the bed, now totally naked. She sat on the edge of the bed and reached her hand out to wrap around his cock. Gently, skillfully, she began moving her hand up and down, sending shivers of sensation through Bob's body. As she leaned over him, her breasts swung forward and her nipples brushed lightly against his skin.

"Close your eyes," she ordered.

"Why?"

"I have a surprise for you. Here, I will kiss them closed."

Bob closed his eyes and felt her lips against the eyelids, first one, then the other. He was drifting in a sea of pleasure.

Then he heard the metallic click as the sear engaged the cylinder and the hammer came back. He felt something cold and hard, and when he opened his eyes he saw that the girl was holding a revolver pointed at his testicles.

"Do not move, señor," she said in a low, flat voice. All the warmth was gone now. "Or you will never enjoy a woman again."

"What the hell is this?" Bob asked, raising up on his elbows. "What are you doing?"

"Ricardo!" the girl called.

The door opened and four men entered the little room. They were all Mexican, and all were smiling.

"Good evening, Señor Depro," one of them said. He sat on the chair and folded his arms across his chest. The men who were with him began tying Bob to the bed. They used leather thongs to secure his wrists to the iron head rail and his ankles to the foot rail.

"Who are you?" Bob asked. "What's going on here?"

"Allow me to introduce myself, señor. I am Ricardo Segura. I have the honor of being a vaquero for Don Juan de la Montoya. These men are riders for Señor Montoya. You are one of the men Señor Elam has hired to make war against Rancho Montoya, yes?"

"I don't know what you're talking about." Bob pulled at his wrists, testing the tie. He was securely bound.

Rosita jammed the barrel of the gun into his balls so hard that it hurt, and he let out a gasp of pain.

"I know it is true, so please do not lie again, señor. My sister would be most happy to shoot the balls off a gringo." He said the same thing again in Spanish for the benefit of the other men and they all laughed uproariously at his joke.

"Your sister?" Bob asked in surprise. "You let your sister sit around naked in front of these men?"

Ricardo shrugged his shoulders and turned the palms of his hands out. "What can I say, señor? My sister is a *puta*, a whore. These men have all known her. Now you will tell the truth. You are one of the men Señor Elam hired to make war against Rancho Montoya, yes?"

"Yes."

"Ah, good, good." Ricardo stood up and looked down at Bob, making his hand into a fist. "I am going to enjoy this," he said as he delivered the first blow.

"Thank you for coming by tonight, Billy Joe," Vi said at the front door of her place. She brushed away an imaginary spot from his shirt. "You must try my pies again."

"It was my pleasure, ma'am," Billy Joe replied.

"No," she said, giggling and brushing against him again. "Believe me, the pleasure was all mine. It's been a long time. Most men stay away from me."

"Maybe they aren't able to handle what you have to offer," Billy Joe suggested.

"I know this, Billy Joe Higgins," Vi said, leaning against him. "It'll be a long time before I find anyone else as able as you."

Billy Joe chuckled, then left the pie shop. Vi closed and locked the door behind him, and by the time Billy Joe was half a block down the street, the shop was totally dark, belying what had just taken place there.

Billy Joe was sometimes teased by the others in the group, because when it came to women, he was basically a shy man. He knew that the average woman was frightened of him. He had learned long ago, however, that big women faced the same problem. Billy Joe never missed a chance to take advantage of the opportunity whenever it presented itself, though he was prone to keep quiet about it. No one would hear about his experience with Vi, because he figured it was nobody's business but his and Vi's.

Billy Joe spent almost fifteen minutes drinking at the bar of the New York Saloon before he learned that Bob wasn't upstairs with a woman.

"You sure he's not up there?" he asked the bartender.

"Mister, there ain't nobody up there like the man you're describin'. You should try that Mex place across the way."

Billy Joe headed over there to find him. He asked the bartender, who nodded toward a pretty Mexican girl sitting at the table near the back wall.

"I am Rosita, señor," the girl said, smiling prettily at him when he went over to her. She leaned over to show her ample cleavage. "Can I do something for you?"

"Señorita, I'm looking for my friend, my *amigo*," he said, using the word he had learned since arriving in Arizona. He described Bob.

"No," she said. "I have not seen anyone like your Amigo. Maybe you like Rosita for yourself, eh?"

Billy Joe sighed and stood up. He decided that the man in the New York Saloon had either lied or made a mistake.

"No, thanks," he said. "I guess I've made a mistake. I'll—" he continued but stopped in midsentence, then went over to another table and picked up a black hat with a red headband. It was one of the first purchases Bob had made with the money they took from Percy Chester. "This is my friend's hat," Billy Joe said. He looked at the girl, then saw her eyes glance almost imperceptibly toward the top of the stairs.

"You are mistaken, señor," she said. "That hat has been here for many days."

"I think I'll just take a look." Billy Joe started for the stairs.

"No!" the girl screamed, moving for the stairs on the run. "Ricardo!" she yelled. She tried to block Billy Joe, but he pushed her aside.

Just as Billy Joe reached the top of the stairs, the first door opened and a Mexican looked out. Quickly he slammed the door and Billy Joe heard the key turning in the lock.

Billy Joe didn't know if this was a shy customer with one of the saloon girls or if Bob was in that room, but he didn't wait to think about it. He raised his foot and kicked in the door. The door, hinges, and frame exploded into the room with a puff of dust from the mud-chinked walls.

"*Dios!*" someone in the room shouted, and Billy Joe saw him start for a pistol that was lying on the bedside table. Billy Joe reached the table in one giant step. The man grabbed the gun just before Billy Joe did, but he never got the chance to use it. Billy Joe picked him up and threw him through the window. The window smashed with a shower of glass, and the man, with the gun still in his hand, screamed as he fell two stories to the ground below.

There were three other men in the room and they started for Billy Joe, thinking to rush him all at once. Billy Joe picked up one over his head and threw him against the wall. The other two turned tail, making for the door at the same time. Unfortunately for them, even with the opening enlarged by Billy Joe's entrance, it wasn't possible for them both to exit simultaneously, until Billy Joe helped them. Bending over to use his head and shoulders as a battering ram, Billy Joe charged across the room at them, roaring like an angry bull. He smashed into them from the rear, popping them through the opening. Both men went flying out into the hall, then flipped over the rail and crashed onto tables below.

Now everyone in Seguines knew exactly what was going on. Frightened for their own safety, they had left the bar and tables, and were now gathered near the front door. Some had already moved into the street, but a few, whose curiosity overcame their fear, stayed just inside and watched as the two came flying off the upstairs landing to crash onto the tables.

Billy Joe hurried back into the room to look for Bob. Bob's eyes were black, his lips were swollen, and there were bruises and scars on his cheeks where he had been beaten. Despite all that, he was smiling broadly at his giant friend.

"Whooee, Billy Joe," Bob said. "You do kick some ass when you get pissed off."

Billy Joe cut the leather thongs that bound Bob to the bed, then, as Bob pulled his clothes on, Billy Joe gave vent to the rest of his anger. He moved down the hallway, kicking in every door to every room, some of which were occupied by the girls and their customers. Then, when they went downstairs, Billy Joe picked up one of Montoya's men and hurled him through the front window.

Scores of people from other cantinas and even from the New York Saloon across the street had joined the patrons of Seguines, standing in the street, watching what was going on. Bob, who had gone after their horses, rode up, leading Billy Joe's animal.

With the sound of smashing and crashing over, an unearthly quiet had settled on the street. No one said a word as Billy Joe mounted, and even as they started riding away the town remained silent as if the slightest sound might cause Billy Joe to come after them.

Bob twisted around in his saddle and looked back at the crowd and the damaged saloon. He chuckled.

"Billy Joe, sure glad you're on our side."

Thirteen

THERE WERE SOME of the riders on the Double X Ranch that the Raiders got along with, and some they did not. Harbin had realized that, and he had moved the Raiders out of the big bunkhouse and into a smaller one that was normally used only during roundup time. This way they had a bunkhouse all to themselves and were able to keep their own hours, sleeping late in the mornings when the regular cowboys were out working, staying out late at night when the regulars were already in bed.

It was not unusual for one or more of them to come in late and wake the others, but when Bob and Billy Joe came into the bunkhouse that night they were both laughing uproariously. Billy Joe lit a lantern.

"What the hell you lighting a lamp for?" Loomis asked. "Can't a fella get any sleep 'round here?"

"You're gonna need some light if you're gonna doctor your brother," Billy Joe said.

"Doctor my brother? What the hell—"

"Take a look at him," Billy Joe said.

Loomis raised up on his elbows and saw his brother's face.

"Holy shit!"

At his exclamation, Marcus and Hank also raised up to see.

"Jesus," Hank said.

"I got beat up," Bob said, laughing.

"Who done it?" Marcus asked.

"Well, I'm trying to tell you," Bob said. He giggled again.

"You drunk?" Hank asked.

"Drunk? No, I only had a few. If you fellas quit interruptin' me, I'll tell you what happened. I went into this Mexican cantina in town, Seguines they call it, and . . . by God, Marcus, they got the best-lookin' Mexican gal workin' there you ever saw in your life, a little ol' gal by the name of Rosita."

"Don't tell me she done this to you," Hank said.

"Rosita? No, all she did was hold a gun to my balls," Bob said. "Her brother and some of his friends done all this."

During Bob's telling, Loomis got out of bed and poured a pan of water. Now he was trying to tend to his brother, but when he touched a cut, Bob jerked back. "Hold still, dammit," Loomis ordered.

"Well be careful, you ain't shoein' a horse."

Gradually, as Loomis doctored his brother, cleaning the cuts and tending to the bruises, Bob managed to tell the story, sometimes getting up from his chair to add embellishments, only to be pushed back down by Loomis.

"And all the while there I was," he concluded, "tied to the bed, naked as a jay bird, watching it all. I tell you I had the best seat in the house."

"I told you that them girls you pick up in bars is trouble," Hank said.

"At least I ain't ever gonna get backshot by some jealous husband," Bob said.

"That ain't no worse than having your balls blowed off in a whorehouse?"

"I guess not. Anyhow, this didn't have anything to do with whorin'. This was because they was ridin' for Montoya."

The sun was barely up the next morning when Loomis went down to the stable and took out the horse he had ridden in the race with Shorty. Since that day, with Harbin's blessing, he had given the horse several early morning workouts, enjoying them as much as the horse did.

Loomis ran the horse on the alkali flats behind the Diablo livery stable. That way he could bring the horse back to the livery after the run, rub him down, then have him back in the Double X remuda before breakfast.

"We'll be there in a minute, horse," Loomis said, leaning over and patting the animal on the neck as he rode into town. "Take it easy—I'll tell you when you can go."

The main street was quiet. He could smell smoke and frying bacon from a few breakfast fires, and he heard a rooster calling the morning. The side door of a house opened and a woman tossed out a pan of water, then slammed the door and went back inside. A dog walked out and looked up at him curiously, trotted alongside for a moment, then went back to his place of rest on the porch of the emporium.

Loomis passed Seguines, saw the broken windows, and recalled Bob's story. He passed the school, then turned toward the livery. When he got to the flats behind the livery, he got down and adjusted the stirrups to the saddle, then climbed back on. He reached down and stroked the horse. "Are you ready, boy?" He slapped his legs against the animal's side and they were off.

The horse burst forward like a cannonball, reaching top speed almost immediately. Loomis bent low over his withers, holding him close, laughing into the rush of wind with the pure thrill of the run, feeling as if he and the horse were one.

Standing against the rail fence behind the livery, just as she had for the last four times Loomis had taken the horse out for its run, was Carlotta Sanchez. The first time she had seen him, two weeks ago, she had looked away quickly, blushing in embarrassment when he waved. The next time she had shyly waved back. On her third time they had spoken, and he told her when he would be out again so she would be certain to be here.

After what happened last night, however, she wasn't certain Loomis would want to speak to her. The incident at Seguines was the talk of Rancho Montoya, and she had seen the men when they returned, barely able to sit on their horses. At first she was afraid that Señor Montoya would be so angry that he would lead his men in an attack on the Double X, but when Montoya found out the entire story, heard how Señor Depro had been tricked, then tied and beaten by four of his vaqueros, he grew very angry.

"We are men of honor," Montoya said. "I am from a long line of noblemen, going back to the days when my ancestors were honored by the king of Spain for their bravery. I will not have my ancestors dishonored by dishonorable men!"

Montoya's angry shouts could be heard all over the hacienda, and servants moved quickly and quietly to avoid his ire. Ricardo Segura and the men who did the terrible beating were dismissed immediately.

Carlotta wanted to tell Loomis of this. She also wanted to tell him something she had learned about Señor Harbin.

Loomis finished the run, then dismounted in front of Carlotta. He smiled at her and patted the horse.

"What do you think?" he asked. "Did he look good today?"

"You were both beautiful," Carlotta said, beaming proudly. She realized then what she said, and she gasped and put her hand over her mouth, blushing furiously.

Loomis looked at her flashing black eyes, her cheeks pinkened from her blush, and at the dimples deepened by her smile.

"Well, now, I don't know as I ever been called that before," he said. "But if they's anyone who should know what the word means, it's a beautiful girl like you."

Carlotta looked down at the ground in embarrassment. She had no experience in flirting or in being flirted with. Her engagement to Esteban had been arranged entirely without courtship. The day she met him was the day they left Mexico to come north on what was to have been their nuptial trip.

"You're out awful early," Loomis said.

Carlotta pointed to the school. "I come early so that I may help Miss Harbin with the younger children."

"Oh," Loomis said. He patted the horse's head and the horse nuzzled up to him.

"He likes you," Carlotta said.

"He's a good horse."

"Loomis," she said. It was the first time she had ever spoken his name, the first time he had heard his name spoken with an accent and it came out "Loo-mees." "I am sorry about what happened to your brother last night."

"Oh. You know about it?"

"*Si*. Everyone on Rancho Montoya knows about it."

"I guess they got a good laugh out of it," Loomis said.

"No, Loomis. The men who did it are gone. Señor Montoya—how you say?—stopped them."

"Fired them?"

"*Si*. Señor Montoya is a man of honor. What these men did was a bad thing."

"Well, don't that beat all," Loomis said. He smiled. "But from what I heard, they already paid a pretty good price for what they did."

"Oh, *si, si*," Carlotta agreed. "They said many men

came from Señor Elam's ranch armed with big sticks."

"Many men?" Loomis laughed. "Wasn't but one man, Carlotta. Billy Joe Higgins did it all by hisself."

"My," Carlotta said. "He is a strong man?"

"Sure is. I can't wait to see the look on Harbin's face this morning when he hears about it."

The smile left Carlotta's face. "Oh, you do not know?" She looked across the street at the schoolhouse. "I do not want to tell Miss Harbin the bad news, but someone must."

"What bad news?"

"Last night, in the village of Naco, Señor Harbin was killed."

"What?" Loomis asked. Of all the men on the Double X Ranch, Harbin was the only one he and the other raiders trusted. "Who did it? Montoya's men?"

"No, señor. That is what is strange. He was killed by the short man . . . who works for Señor Elam."

"Mason?"

"*Si*. Mason."

"But they're on the same side."

"One of Señor Montoya's vaqueros was in Naco visiting his cousin. He was in the cantina when it happened and he told us everything. Señor Elam was meeting with General Pedro Bustamante. When Senor Harbin saw them, Señor Elam then told the short man to kill him."

"I'll be damned," Loomis said. He patted the horse on the neck, then remembered that it was Harbin who gave him permission to give the animal his workouts.

"Today Señor Elam will bring Señor Harbin's body back. I am sure he will tell a story that is different and I am sure all the gringos will believe him. But, believe me when I say this, Loomis," she said and put her hand on his arm and looked at him with her deep, dark eyes. "Señor Elam is a man of evil."

"Well, honey, I ain't no angel," Loomis said, smiling. "So if I'm gonna run with the likes of Ike Elam, they ain't nothin' gonna rub off on me, you can count on that."

"I am worried, Loomis," Carlotta said. She turned away with a tear squeezing from the corner of her eye.

"Shit!" Loomis said. He reached for her and pulled her to him, then kissed her soundly on the lips. She gasped in surprise and stood there for a moment with her eyes wide open. Then, as the feelings gradually began spreading through her, she put her arms around his neck and leaned into him, pressing her young body against him.

"I'll bet you're a virgin, too."

"*Si*," she said proudly.

"Uh-huh, that's what I thought." Loomis extricated himself gently, then mounted the horse. He had planned to rub him down here, but he felt he should get back to the ranch. "Listen, girl, I'm thinkin' you better find someone else to be interested in. I ain't no good for you."

Loomis clicked at the horse and rode away at a brisk trot, leaving Carlotta standing behind, tears streaming down her face.

* * *

Marcus rode into Diablo as soon as Loomis told him the news about Harbin. Julie had already been told about her father by Carlotta, and a few of the parents of her children were there, offering what comfort they could. When she saw Marcus standing just inside the door of the school, she excused herself and came back to see him.

"Thank you for coming, Marcus," she said.

"I wasn't sure you'd want to see me," Marcus replied. "Seems to me like you been doin' what you could to avoid me ever since I got here."

"I know," Julie said. "That was wrong of me. I hope you forgive me for being so foolish."

"Ain't nothin' to forgive."

Julie looked back into the classroom at the people who had gathered to comfort her. They were standing in little groups, talking quietly, wondering who the man was.

"Where is your father now?"

"He is down at the undertaker's. Mr. Nunlee asked if I wanted . . ." she said and choked back a sob. "If I wanted to display the deceased. I told him no. The last time I saw my father he had a smile on his face. That is how I want to remember him."

"Your father was a good man," Marcus said. "Don't seem to be too many of that breed out here."

"Marcus, I wish you weren't riding for Ike Elam."

"Julie, your father was the one hired us to ride for Elam."

"I know. But Elam hired Mason, and Mason is the one who killed my father."

"They say it was a fair fight," Marcus said.

"A fair fight? Between my father and Mason?"

Marcus pinched the bridge of his nose, then sighed.

"You're right," he said. "Anyway, I went lookin' for Mason after I found out about it. I wanted to hear his side of it, but he run off."

"Elam fired him," Julie said. "He told me that when he told me what happened."

"If he's still around, I'll find him."

"And what? Kill him?"

"He's a man that needs killin'," Marcus said matter-of-factly.

Julie closed her eyes tightly, but the tears rolled down anyway. Finally she spoke in a low voice that was full of pain.

"Go away, Marcus," she said.

"What?"

"Please, just go away. Can't you see? You're a part of it . . . all this violence. Where does it end? Mason pulled the trigger, Elam hired him, but everywhere I look you and your friends are right in the middle. I'm foolish to be grieving for my father. I should have known a long time ago that this was going to happen."

"Julie, I didn't start things out here, and it ain't gonna change just 'cause you want it to."

"Please," she said, "just go."

Marcus shook his head slowly and walked away.

Fourteen

SINCE JIM HARBIN was not a man who often went to church, Julie thought a church funeral would be inappropriate. However, she did ask the town's only Protestant parson to conduct the service and he agreed. Ike Elam offered to have the funeral at the Double X Ranch, but Julie declined. The funeral was held in the schoolhouse where Julie not only taught, but would now live.

Carlotta had reported to Julie what she had heard about the gunfight that killed her father. Julie, in turn, asked Ike Elam for his own version of what happened, and he stood in the back of the classroom while the mourners were filing in and told her his side of the story.

"In the first place, like I said at the beginnin', it was a fair fight. But I won't have a man who settles all disagreements with a pistol. That's why I fired him."

"But I don't understand," Julie said. "What on earth would cause my father to get into a gunfight with a known gunfighter? My father was no coward, but he was a sensible man, and a sensible man does not challenge a professional gunfighter."

"It all had to do with who was boss," Elam explained. "You see, Mason reckoned that since he was my bodyguard, he didn't have to take no order from your father. But Jim was a proud man who figured that everyone on this ranch, except me, come under his orders. I agreed with your father, but I could see that Mason was bein' pushed."

"Then why didn't you stop it?"

"I tried to, Julie, believe me," Elam said. "First I tried to get your father to get on his horse and leave. Everyone in the cantina heard me tell him to ride away. I hoped he would do so, then return when tempers had cooled. When he wouldn't do that, I told Mason to take care of it."

"Take care of it? What did you mean by that?" That was the same expression that was reported to her by Carlotta.

"I wanted him to settle it," Elam explained. "When I saw that the only way he intended to settle it was with a gun, and when I saw that your father had no intention of riding away, I did the only thing I could think of, and that was furnish your father with a gun."

"You . . . you gave him the gun he used?"

"Of course I did," Elam said.

"But why? If he hadn't had a gun, he couldn't have had the fight."

"Julie, your father was my friend. I wasn't going to

stand by and watch him get shot down in cold blood. I figured he ought to at least have the chance to defend himself. I mean, you understand that, don't you?"

"I . . . I don't know," Julie said. She had to admit that, in a terrible, tragic way, everything Elam was saying to her made sense. Perhaps the Mexican who reported his version of the fight to Carlotta was wrong.

After the funeral, Julie stood at his graveside for a long time, even after the others had gone, and looked at the pile of dirt that the gravediggers were throwing down on her father. She had wept bitter tears of grief for the past three days, but now her eyes were dry and her sorrow was numbed. There remained only anger at the brutal and senseless killing. Finally she left the cemetery. Her father was buried here in Diablo, her mother back in Texas. She was alone now, but she had her job as a schoolteacher, her friends, and, in the little room at the back of the schoolhouse, she had a place to stay. She'd make her own way. She knew her father would want that.

One week later, under the auspices of conducting a scout to look for any Montoya riders who might be on Double X land, Quinn and the others pushed the first group of cows they had rounded up toward the Mexican border. There they would sell them to Colonel Morales, the corrupt Mexican officer with whom Hank had made contact. The herd consisted of twelve steers from Rancho Montoya.

In truth, however, only nine of the Double X cows were animals that were recovered from Rancho

Montoya. Marcus wanted an even dozen, so the Raiders just stole three more head from Elam's herd. They didn't like Elam, or anyone who worked for him, so the hell with him. It was business, pure and simple.

But it might not be as easy as they'd planned. Ever since they'd left the box canyon, Marcus had been aware that several men were dogging them, riding parallel, and, for the most part, staying out of sight. They were good, but Marcus was better. He was on to them as soon as they started shadowing the trail.

Marcus moved up alongside Hank.

"Do you see them?" he asked.

"I make eight so far," Hank answered.

"I've got ten," Marcus replied. "There's two more ridin' ahead of the main bunch."

"Who are they?" Hank asked.

"Shorty's one of the two up ahead," Marcus said. "Looks like maybe we been caught with our hand in the till."

"Think the law's with 'em?"

"No. I reckon Shorty's got it in mind he'd like to take care of this hisself . . . make him look like a hero to Elam."

"Where you figure they'll hit us?"

"Shorty ain't showed up in the notch of that hill off to our left yet. I figure he'll try an' set up an ambush right there."

"What you got in mind?"

"Same as usual. Tell the boys to be ready to move on my signal."

"Right," Hank said, slapping his legs against the

side of his horse and sloping off down the hill toward Bob.

Shorty held up his hand and the others stopped.

"They'll be comin' through this pass any time now," he said, pointing to a notch between two hills. "When they do we'll shoot 'em down like dogs."

"Shorty, don't you think maybe we ought to just ride on back an' tell Deekus?" one of the others asked.

"Why?" Shorty asked. "Elam made Deekus his foreman after Harbin got hisself kilt, when Deekus never done nothin' to prove he should'a got the job. Then he run Mason off, and now these here five ex-Rebs he's payin' all that money is stealin' from him. Well, when I bring 'em back slung over the saddle you better believe Elam's gonna take another look at ol' Shorty. I'm gonna be sittin' high in the catbird seat, an' when I am, I'm gonna take care of my friends. I ain't gonna be like Deekus, an' forget ever'one in the bunkhouse I used to ride with. Now you fellas with me or not?"

"Yeah, we're with you," one of them said.

"Good. I only got one request. Don't nobody shoot that little shit. Leave him to me."

"You mean the one beat you in the race?"

"Cheated me," Shorty said hotly. "Only, when I get through with him, he ain't gonna ever cheat nobody again." Shorty looked at the nine men he had with him, then at the little opening where Quinn and the others would appear. All of his men were well armed, well mounted, and concealed. They'd shoot Quinn and the others down before they knew what hit them.

Shorty cocked his pistol and stared straight ahead. The first cow came through the pass and he waited. The next cow came, then the next and the next. Within the space of a moment, all twelve cows had passed through the space, and yet not one rider was with them.

"Shorty, where the hell are they?" someone called up to him.

Shorty stood up and looked down toward the pass in confusion. He scratched his head.

"Hello, Shorty," Marcus called down to them. "You lookin' for us?"

Marcus and the Raiders had left the herd as soon as it was behind the hill. Then, riding hard and staying in defilade, they had rounded the hill to come up behind anyone who might be watching them. By the time the herd was in view, Marcus and his men were already in position, watching as Shorty and the others readied their guns.

"The sons of bitches are behind us!" Shorty shouted, then raised his rifle and fired.

Marcus's horse reared, then fell, and Marcus had to roll to one side to avoid being crushed. He leaped to his feet and tried to catch the horse, but it darted away, leaving Marcus afoot, his pistol in his hand.

One of the Double X riders galloped toward him, smiling broadly at the prospect of an easy kill. Marcus fired and the cowboy pitched out of his saddle. There was no cover and Marcus was out in the open, unmounted, not a good place to be. Another horseman loomed on his right. Marcus fired again. His bullet hit the horse and it stumbled, throwing the rider over his head.

Bob galloped up to him, holding his hand down to help Marcus mount behind him. Marcus leaped onto the horse and the two men galloped to the cover of a nearby group of rocks. Marcus slid down then and ran to one of the rocks as a bullet whistled by his ear. He squeezed off another shot and saw a hat fly.

Hank, Loomis, and Billy Joe came to join him then. Hank's shotgun and Billy Joe's Mare's Leg roared like miniature cannons, and as the smoke billowed out before them, the place began to look like a battlefield.

Shorty, who had planned to get himself promoted to foreman over this, suddenly realized that most of his men were gone, either lying dead in the dirt or riding off somewhere, carrying lead and bleeding from their wounds. Enraged at the way things turned out, he stood and yelled toward the rocks where Quinn's Raiders had taken shelter.

"Loomis Depro!" he called.

"I'm here," Loomis called down to him.

"Let's have it out, boy. Me an' you." Shorty put his pistol in his holster and held his arms out by his sides.

Loomis slipped his own pistol into his holster, then stepped out from behind the rock.

Shorty looked at Loomis for a long moment, his eyes glowering with hate. Blood was running down his forehead from a nick on the top of the head.

"Boy, you're a cheatin', no-good son of a bitch," Shorty said. "You didn't beat me fair an' square."

"Shorty, I could'a beat you if I'd rode a mule," Loomis said.

With a yell of defiance, Shorty went for his pistol. Although Loomis wasn't the fastest of the Raiders, he was quick, and he had his pistol out in the blink of an eye. Despite that, Shorty still managed to get off the first shot, though as it was hurried, the bullet whizzed by, doing no damage. Loomis returned fire and his bullet hit Shorty in the chest, knocking him backwards. Loomis held the smoking gun in his hand, ready to fire again, but Shorty lay dead with a single bullet in his heart. Loomis holstered his pistol and looked at the others.

"Little brother, I'd say that man was a sore loser," Bob said, looking toward Shorty's body.

The impromptu battlefield was silent now, and the boys looked out over what they had done. Besides Shorty, five of the men who had been with him were dead. Four others, carrying lead, had ridden off.

"Shit," Marcus said.

"What is it?" Hank asked.

"The goddamned cows scattered."

"We gonna chase 'em down?"

Marcus took his hat off and rubbed his hand through his hair. He was hot, tired, sweaty, and still edgy from the gunfight.

"Boys," he finally said, "I'll be damned if I'm gonna gallop all over hell and back trying to round up a bunch of cows. Ain't worth the worry now."

"They do seem spread thin for miles," Hank said, looking out over open country past the hills. "Gunplay scared them good."

"Amen to that," Hank said, laughing. "Looks like we're out of the rustling business. Yeah, and we ain't cowboys anyways," Billy Joe added.

"Somebody get my horse," Marcus said, who looked at the others as Loomis mounted and started after Quinn's horse. "I reckon when the others get back to the ranch, we won't have a job with Elam, neither."

"You got any ideas?"

"What if we try the grass on the other side of the fence for a while?"

"You mean work for Montoya?" Bob asked.

"Something like that. You got a problem with that on account of you gettin' beat up like you done?"

"Well, I ain't gonna go over there an' kiss the Mexican bastards if that's what you mean," Bob said. Then he smiled. "But if I'm on their side, maybe Rosita will be more friendly."

Fifteen

WHEN THE BOYS rode into Diablo that night it was raining. The rain blew against the windows and drummed on the roofs. It turned the streets of the little town into muddy rivers. On the range, cattle moved instinctively to higher ground and the desert creatures abandoned their holes to wait out the downpour. In addition to the rain there were great, jagged sheets of lightning, shards of light that zigzagged down from the sky to be followed immediately by the cannonading of thunder, booming at first, then rolling back as a distant, rumbling echo from the nearby hills.

In view of the fact that the boys had been caught stealing Double X cattle, they figured they should avoid the New York Saloon. They also figured they had better make a few connections with the Mexicans, if they wanted to work for Montoya, so they found a cantina where they could keep themselves dry on the outside and wet on the inside.

Just down the street from the cantina, in her room at the rear of the schoolhouse, Julie had already gone to bed. She lay there listening to the rain, watching the flashes of lightning through the window, shrinking before the crashing reports of thunder. Then, in between the thunder and the roar of rain, she heard a banging sound from the front of the schoolhouse. She lay there for a full moment longer, trying to ignore it, but she knew she couldn't. If it were the door, she would have to close it right away. She couldn't afford to have her books ruined by the rain. With a sigh Julie got up to go investigate.

At first she thought she would take a candle. Then she decided she didn't want to waste the match. Besides, she knew the classroom so well that she could navigate it with her eyes closed.

The thunder boomed and the rain roared as she walked from her room, through the children's cloak room, and out into the classroom. She stayed against the wall and started toward the front door.

Suddenly she stopped.

She hadn't heard or seen anything, but she had the most terrifying, cloying sensation that she wasn't alone. She felt her hair stand on end and a hollowness develop in the pit of her stomach.

"Hello?" she called out tentatively. She waited for a moment but got no answer. "Hello, who's here?" she called again. Still no answer. The feeling grew stronger. "I know someone is here," she said, her voice nearly breaking. "Who is it? What do you want? If you're just looking to get out of the rain, please tell me. You are frightening me."

Suddenly there was a brilliant flash of lightning, a large bolt that illuminated everything for fully two seconds. The entire classroom was brightly lit, a world without color. She could see every object in the room with amazing clarity. She saw each desk standing out in bold relief, the day's homework assignment still written on the blackboard.

And she could see Mason, standing just inside the door, a hideous smile on his face.

The room went instantly black. Julie screamed, but it was drowned out by the crash of thunder that came immediately after the light died.

"Come here, bitch!" Mason shouted. He started to run toward her, but in the dark he hit his shin and tripped over one of the desks. He fell, cursing, to the floor.

Julie turned to run but stopped short. She couldn't go to her room because there was no door leading out and she would be trapped there. The only way out of the building was the front door, but she couldn't get to it without passing Mason.

She got down on her hands and knees and crawled quickly along the floor just below the blackboard to hide behind her desk. She had to think. She couldn't just go pell-mell around the room. She remembered that there was a loose board right there, so she moved around it, then crawled on to the opposite wall.

"Where are you, whore," Mason said. "I've got something for you." He giggled insanely. Another flash of lightning, neither as brilliant nor as long as the previous flash, lit the room dimly. From her position on the floor behind her desk, Julie could see that Mason was now holding a gun.

The light frightened her and she moved sharply, bumping into a book chest. Mason heard her and looked over just as the light was dying. He got a fleeting glimpse of her and he fired, the flash from his pistol illuminating the room for a split second.

The bullet crashed into the chest near her and splinters of wood flew around the room. One little sliver hit her in the arm and she felt its sting.

"Make it easy for me and I'll make you like it," Mason called. He began moving, stumbling into one desk after another, cursing with each new obstacle.

Julie crawled quickly along the far wall, heading toward the door.

"I made it easy for your papa," Mason said. "I killed him quick. I could do the same for you . . . after," he added, sliding out the last word so that she knew what it meant.

Julie crawled another few feet; then she knocked a book off a nearby desk. It fell with a loud thud.

Mason fired again, this time at the sound, and she felt the bullet whiz by, frying the air just in front of her, before it slammed into the wall.

"I can kill you first," Mason said. "'Course, you'd like it better iffen I'd let you live for a while, but it don't make me no never mind."

Julie moved back a little.

"What are you trying to do, girl? Make it to the door?" Mason started moving again and Julie could hear that he was headed for the door. "Yeah, you do that. You try an' make it to the door. I'll just be here waitin' on you."

DIABLO DOUBLE CROSS

Another streak of lightning, the room flashed white, and she could see him standing no more than ten feet from her. He was looking around, fortunately in the wrong direction, so he didn't see her. The room grew dark again and the thunder rumbled.

In the cantina, Marcus was sitting around the table with the others, discussing the difference between tequila and Tennessee sour mash. Because of the thunder and rain, Marcus wasn't sure he had heard the first shot. But when he heard it again, he knew what it was, and he stood up and walked to the door, curious about what it could be. This was not the kind of night to be firing a pistol in drunken revelry.

From the front door of the cantina, Marcus looked out across the rain-swept street at the gray buildings on the other side when he heard the third gunshot, and, out of the corner of his eye, saw the flash of red from inside the schoolhouse. Now he knew where it was coming from, and he ran out into the rain to check it out.

Julie crawled backward so she wouldn't be where she was when he saw her. She felt along the wall, feeling the art shelf where she kept the rulers, paste, watercolors, scissors, and compass, the little device her kids used for making circles. She realized that she was only about ten feet from the door. Ten feet, so agonizingly close, yet so terrifyingly far. If only she could distract him, get him to turn his attention away from the door. She felt through the art shelf until she found a jar of paste.

"Come on, bitch," Mason called to her. "I'm really

gettin' tired of all this. You'd make it so much easier if you'd just give yourself up. The longer you make me wait the worse it's gonna be."

Julie tossed the jar across the room, and Mason fired toward the sound. When he did, she got up and ran toward the front door, but he saw her in the muzzle flash, and he ran to the door and grabbed her. She screamed.

"Now, bitch!" Mason said. "I got you now!"

They were standing in the front door, within inches of escaping him. The door was wide open and rain was blowing in, soaking her nightgown, plastering her hair to the side of her face.

There was another brilliant flash of lightning, and Julie saw Marcus Quinn standing in the street, his gun in his hand, his arm down by his side. He looked like an angel from hell, oblivious to the rain, ankle deep in mud, with a face fully as frightening as the face of the man who held her.

"Let her go, Mason!" Quinn called.

Mason jumped in surprise, but instead of letting her go, he tightened his grip.

"That you, Quinn?"

"It's me."

"You'd better back on out of this," he said. "It ain't none of your business."

"No," Quinn said. "I'm makin' this my business."

Mason twisted around so that he was holding Julie as his shield.

"They ain't nothin' you can do about it without hittin' the girl," he said.

"You can't stand there and hold her all night,"

Marcus said. "You got to let her go sometime, an' when you do, I'm gonna kill you."

"Not if I kill you first!" Mason shouted, firing at the sound of the voice. He fired just over Julie's shoulder. Her face burned with spent powder, her ears rung with the explosion. In the muzzle flash she saw Marcus leap to one side.

There was another lightning flash at that instant and Mason was startled by it. He released his grip slightly, and Julie threw herself off the side of the front porch into a mud puddle.

"Marcus!" she heard herself shout.

Almost on top of her voice she heard two guns roar as Mason and Marcus fired together. For an instant she was frozen in fear as she had no idea of the outcome. Then she heard Mason's gun clatter to the wooden deck of the front porch. After that, Mason himself collapsed. With a shout of relief she ran toward Marcus and, in the mud and water-soaked nightgown, threw herself into his arms.

Sixteen

AS USUAL, CARLOTTA was the first person to arrive at school the next morning. Although most of the water had receded in the street, there were still mud puddles here and there. Carlotta had to pick her way carefully from the buckboard to the schoolhouse. She held her skirt high to avoid muddying the hem, then stepped across one last puddle to the wooden steps. Once inside the building, she saw that the rain had soaked the floor and even some of the books. Clucking her tongue quietly, she began moving the books to a place where they could dry.

"Miss Harbin," she said, starting toward Julie's room in the back of the school. "I'm going to put these books out to dry, so if you—" She stopped in midsentence with a gasp. She had just pushed Julie's door open, as she had many times before. But this time she saw Miss Harbin in bed with Marcus Quinn.

Julie woke up when she heard Carlotta gasp, then, realizing that she was naked, and in bed with a naked man, she knew what must be going through Carlotta's mind. She pulled the cover up to her chin.

"Please, forgive me," Carlotta apologized, so embarrassed by her discovery that she could scarcely speak. She turned and ran back into the classroom.

"No, Carlotta! Carlotta, wait!" Julie called, and she got up, wrapping a sheet around her. "Carlotta, listen, please!"

Carlotta stopped at the front of the room.

"Don't go," Julie asked in a quiet voice.

"I should not open your door," the young girl said.

"Please, wait a minute," Julie said. She hurried back into her room and put on a robe, then walked back out into the classroom where she saw Carlotta was picking up books.

"The rain," Carlotta said. "It has made a mess."

"No, it wasn't the rain. Look." Julie pointed to the holes in the book chest, then to a hole in the wall. "These are bullet holes."

"Bullet holes?"

Quickly Julie explained what happened the previous night, how Mason had come to the school to terrorize her, and how, like an avenging angel arriving on a bolt of lightning, Marcus Quinn had come to save her.

"You don't need to say more," Carlotta said, smiling. "I will say nothing."

"Miss Harbin and I 'ppreciate that," a man's voice said, and Carlotta and Julie looked around to see Marcus standing in the door that led to Julie's room.

He had on his shirt and trousers and was putting on his boots.

"I am grateful to you for saving my teacher, señor," Carlotta said.

"Grateful enough to speak for me to Señor Montoya?"

"Speak for you in what way?"

"I would like to offer him a deal," Marcus said.

"And what of Loomis?" Carlotta asked.

Marcus looked at Carlotta with an expression of surprise on his face, then he grinned knowingly. "Yes, Loomis, too."

Carlotta smiled broadly, happily. "*Si*, I will speak for you."

"Why do you no longer wish to work for Señor Elam?" Montoya asked.

"We wasn't hired by Elam—we was hired by Harbin. With him dead I don't figure we owe Elam anything. Besides which, I sort'a figure Elam had somethin' to do with killin' Harbin, and maybe somethin' to do with tryin' to kill Miss Harbin last night," Marcus explained.

"Yes, Carlotta told me that you saved Miss Harbin's life. My people like Miss Harbin very much," Montoya said. "If all gringos were like her, there would be no war between us. But what work would you do for me? I do not want a private army, señor. If I had wanted one, I would have hired Bustamante."

"No private army," Marcus said. "Just a little roundup, is all. We'll go over to Double X and round up any of your cows that might'a strayed over there. For that, we want five dollars a head."

"You want me to buy my own cows back for five dollars a head?"

"You ain't buyin' 'em back, you're givin' a reward for 'em," Marcus said.

Montoya looked at Marcus through stern eyes for a long moment. "Señor Quinn, you and your friends are brave men to make such an offer to me. I am sorry, but I must refuse. We will deal with Señor Elam in our own way. But for now, please accept my hospitality until you are ready to leave Diablo."

Marcus smiled and stuck out his hand. "Much obliged. On behalf of my boys here, we accept."

The piano was playing merrily, but the saloon was so noisy that the people twenty feet away from the piano couldn't hear a note. In one corner a group of raucous men started their own singing in competition with the piano. Included in the group were Deekus and Curly.

"Hey, Curly," Deekus said when the singing was over. "You seem to be in an awfully good mood."

"Why not?" someone asked. "Ever since Shorty got hisself shot, ol' Curly here figures he's second man on the totem pole."

"You're a man of mighty strong ambition to be celebratin' the killin' of a friend," Deekus said.

Curly snorted. "Son of a bitch weren't no friend of mine. We just worked together, that's all."

"Anyhow, who said you were next in line?" Deekus asked.

"Nobody told me. Nobody had to. I been here the longest—that makes me next."

"Not 'less you do somethin' to prove you deserve it."

"What you want me to do?"

"Well, for starters, maybe you could slip out to Montoya's place an' find out what Quinn an' his bunch is up to."

"A fella could get hisself killed that way," Curly said.

"He could," Deekus agreed. "He could also prove he deserves to be the number-two ramrod."

"Don't know," Curly hedged.

"'Course, I understand you bein' afraid to go," Deekus taunted.

Curly wasn't sure that Deekus was serious. Deekus sometimes taunted people, just for fun, and he suspected that's what he was doing now. Still, if he could go out there and find out what Quinn and the others were up to, it sure would put him in real good with Elam. He said nothing, but he made up his mind that he would go out there that night.

It was easy enough to slip onto Montoya's land. All Curly had to do was wear a sombrero and serape and in the dark no one would ever notice the difference. He passed by half a dozen people without once being stopped or even looked at very closely. Dumb-ass Mexicans, he thought.

The great hacienda was well lit with bright, golden light spilling out of every window. He rode around to the barn, thinking to watch from there until he figured out what to do next.

Curly heard a familiar laugh and he froze. He

looked toward the bunkhouse and saw that it was as well lit as the big house. The laugh he heard was the heavy, booming laugh of Billy Joe Higgins. Curly, like everyone else, had heard the story of Billy Joe Higgins wrecking the cantina.

He heard another laugh; this time it was Hank's. He breathed easier. They were probably all in there with the Mexicans, drinking tequila and playing cards. They might even be drunk by now and if so, that would make it easier for him to poke around without being seen.

Curly heard someone coming and he stepped back into the shadows of the barn. When he peered around the corner he saw the pretty young girl who had been helping out Harbin's daughter at the school. The girl was carrying a dark-colored shirt with her, and when she reached the stall of the chestnut horse on the end, Curly recognized that horse. Loomis must have stolen it when he left the Double X. He'd have to tell Deekus.

The pretty Mexican girl draped the shirt she was carrying across the stall, then began removing the colorfully beaded blouse she was wearing.

"Hello, horse," she said. "Do you wish a rubdown? I will rub you down as soon as I change my blouse. This is not a blouse to wear for working."

Curly watched as the girl took off the blouse. In the dim spill of light from outside, he could see her breasts—firm, proud, upturned, and naked. His breath shortened and he felt sweat on the palms of his hands. He hadn't planned on this, but this was too good an opportunity to pass up. He looked around to make sure no one else was around. When he was certain it was clear, he slipped in behind her.

The girl heard him and she stiffened, her arm frozen in the act of reaching for the other shirt. "Loomis?" the girl called softly. "Loomis, is that you?"

"Naw, it ain't Loomis, little girl. It's a real man."

Carlotta gasped in fear, then turned, her hand raised to her mouth. "Who are you?" she asked. "What do you want?"

"Well, now, you know what I want," Curly said, opening his pants as he grabbed her and threw her to the ground in one of the stalls, then jerked her skirt down. She tried to fight against him, but he was too strong for her. She closed her eyes tight and prepared for the worst.

Suddenly Carlotta heard a dull thump and a groan of pain and opened her eyes to see Curly rolling across the ground. Loomis was standing over her, glaring at Curly with eyes that were narrow slits of killing rage.

As quick as a cat, Curly leaped to his feet. That was when Carlotta saw the knife in his hand, low and menacing, the point weaving back and forth like the head of a snake.

"Well, now, kid," Curly hissed. "It's one thing to ride a horse ag'in a full-grown man. But this here's a fight—a man's fight, sonny."

Curly lunged toward Loomis, swinging his hand before him in a wide, slashing arc. Loomis let Curly charge, then at the last minute, ducked sharply. Curly recovered quickly and turned back for him. Loomis still had no weapon.

Carlotta had regained her feet by now, and she started to run for help when she saw an awl that had been used to work some leather. She grabbed the awl and held it toward Loomis. Loomis saw it and signaled her to toss it to him. She did, and he caught it cleanly by the handle.

The sudden appearance of a weapon in his hand startled Curly and he stopped in midcharge. That gave Loomis the split-second opening he needed and he stabbed forward with the awl, penetrating Curly's flesh just between the fifth and sixth ribs. Curly let out a surprised gasp and dropped his knife. Loomis twisted and gouged, making certain the wound was fatal, and he watched as the life left Curly's eyes. When he backed away a second later he let go of the awl and Curly fell dead before he even hit the ground.

A few hours later Quinn and his Raiders rode into town. They rode down the dark street to the front of the New York Saloon; then Marcus fired a pistol in the air.

"Deekus! Deekus, you in there?"

The piano music and most of the noise stopped. There was a scuffling of feet as the patrons hurried to the bat-wing doors and looked outside to see what was going on. Deekus pushed his way through the crowd.

"Who's callin' me?"

"Marcus Quinn. I've got something for you."

"Deekus, that there's Curly," someone said, noticing a sixth horse with a body draped over the saddle.

"Drop 'im, Loomis," Marcus ordered.

Loomis reached over and gave the body a push. Curly slid off his saddle and fell to the street.

"You kill 'im?" Deekus asked.

"I did," Loomis said.

"Thieving bastard!"

"We've got a message for your boss from Señor Montoya," Marcus added.

"What's the Mexican have to say?"

"He says there's been too much killin'. He wants to find a way out, and he wants to meet with Elam noon tomorrow."

"You gonna be there with him?" Deekus asked.

"No," Marcus said. "No, we don't want nothin' to do with any of it no more. We're ridin' out of here tonight."

"Wait. Where is this meetin'?"

"Adobe Springs way station," Marcus said. He turned his horse and clucked to it, and the five men rode away, leaving Curly dead in the dirt behind them.

Seventeen

BEHIND MARCUS, THE horizon showed a thin line of gray. In half an hour it would be light enough to see.

Marcus had been truthful with Deekus when he told him that he and his men weren't working for Montoya. But the idea for a peace meeting was part of his plan. He and the others had decided last night that they were ready to ride on. But they didn't want to leave a job half done. They talked about it for a while, then came up with a plan that they thought would work.

The plan depended upon Elam believing that Montoya was really going to meet him at Adobe Springs . . . and it also depended upon Elam double-crossing Montoya in the process.

After they left Diablo, Marcus and the Raiders went straight to Adobe Springs. During the night he heard the sounds of several horses and men. With the soft, gray light of early morning, he could see that Bustamante and at least ten of his men were in position in the rocks around Adobe Springs, set up for the perfect ambush when Montoya arrived. So the wily Mexican general had been in cahoots with Elam all along.

Bustamante's men weren't the only ones in position for the ambush. Marcus had sent Hank and Loomis up the butte behind Bustamante's left flank, and Bob and Billy Joe up the butte behind Bustamante's right flank. Marcus himself was in position behind the old abandoned way station, ready to direct his fire where need be to keep the pot boiling.

Marcus saw a wisp of dust on the horizon and knew that Elam was on his way. So far, so good. Everything was still working perfectly. He looked up to his left and saw Hank, and waved, giving Hank the signal. Then, looking up to his right, he gave the same signal to Bob. The Raiders dug in and waited.

From Marcus's position, he could see every one of Bustamante's men. Just before dawn they had built a fire for their breakfast, and now a few of them were eating beans and tortillas from their positions behind the rocks. A short time later, the cooking fire had been extinguished, and now not even the tiniest wisp of smoke curled up from where the fire had been.

Marcus had to give them credit. They had set up the perfect ambush. If Montoya really were going to come, he would have ridden right into it.

A group of riders appeared below the dust cloud and Marcus lay on his stomach and pushed the Henry rifle in front of him. He levered in a round and waited. The group of riders finally drew close enough for him to identify them. Ike Elam was leading them, as he knew he would be. Alongside Elam was Deekus and nearly a dozen others.

Elam led the group all the way into the pass, then started pointing out rocks and positions of cover around the area.

"Deekus, you get over there," Elam's voice carried up to Marcus. "When I give the word, start blasting away. I want Montoya and everyone with him killed."

"Right, boss. I just wish that goddamn Quinn and his bunch were with them."

"They'll be taken care of," Elam promised. "Soon's word gets out that they ambushed Montoya and killed all his men, they'll be wanted for murder. There won't be noplace they can go without a price on their heads."

Deekus chuckled. "I gotta hand it to you, boss. You're pretty smart."

Marcus drew a bead on Elam's chest. He could drop him from this distance and Elam would never know what hit him. It wasn't a very sporting way to kill a man.

Marcus held that position for a long moment, not quite ready to kill a man from ambush. Then he recalled Shiloh and the job his commander had given him to do. He had lost track of the number of men he killed in that battle, and none of them ever saw the man who killed them. They had been good men— soldiers who were fighting for what they believed in. It just so happened they were wearing a different color uniform, so Marcus killed them. If he could kill decent men in such a way, he should have no compunctions about squeezing the trigger on this bastard.

"Fuck you, Elam," Marcus said under his breath.

The rifle barked and kicked back against his shoulder. He saw a puff of dust rise from Elam's chest, saw the ranch owner raise his hands in surprise, then fall off his horse.

Marcus's shot was the signal for the others and they opened fire on Elam's riders. With their leader down, Elam's men scattered. They started shooting back, and just as Marcus had planned, Bustamante's men, caught up in the crossfire, began shooting back at Elam's men.

Marcus and the Raiders alternated every other shot, firing some at Double X riders and some at Bustamante's banditos. Neither group had yet figured out what was happening to them. The Double X men saw Mexicans, and thought Montoya was here first. All Bustamante's men knew was that the gringos had opened fire on them, and they figured they had been double crossed. A full-scale battle began.

Marcus held his fire for a few moments, watching the effect of the battle. He saw three Double X riders start up the side of the mountain toward the banditos, only to be cut down by Bustamante's men. Then he saw two of Bustamante's men try to improve their position, only to be killed by Double X men. Rifle fire rippled back and forth, then rolled back as echoes as the men killed each other. He heard screams of pain, curses of fury, and he saw men crumple, grabbing their guts, or falling back with holes in their heads, dead before they hit the ground.

Marcus looked up toward Hank and Loomis and

when he caught their attention, he gave them a prearranged signal. A moment later he managed to give the same signal to Bob and Billy Joe. He had made arrangements to meet them on the other side of the north butte, and now he slipped away to keep the rendezvous. All five raiders managed to leave the battle they precipitated without being observed. An hour later they were on the other side of the butte, nearly a mile away from Adobe Springs. They could still hear the rifle fire, though the intensity of the shooting was considerably less than it had been.

"When I left there were only three of Bustamante's men still alive," Bob said.

"How about Bustamante?" Marcus asked.

"He was one of the first to go down."

"I saw you get Elam," Hank said. "It was a damn good shot. I don't think there are more than two or three of his men left alive."

"I reckon this range war is over," Loomis said.

"What now?" Billy Joe asked.

Marcus uncorked his canteen and took a drink of water, then wiped the back of his hand across his mouth. Pushing his hat back off his eyes, he looked toward the open country to the north and nodded.

"Boys, I say we head north—see what we find."

"Can't be no worse than what we just got out of," Billy Joe said.

"You got that right, Billy Joe," Hank added, and the others laughed.

"What about the women back at Diablo?" Loomis asked.

"Send 'em a wire!" Marcus shouted and spurred his mount forward, the other men close behind.

Ride with Marcus Quinn and his tough band of outlaws as they run up against some murdering railroad men and their hired guns out to swindle a whole Nevada town out of their land rights in the next action-packed adventure:

Watch for

Blood Money

*next in the
Quinn's Raiders
series coming in October
from Lynx!*